CHIPPEWA SUNS

31 Aug 2017

Dearest Mary Ann,
   Stopped by to see you and so sorry I missed you. You are so one of my favorite people and I love to visit with you. I

CHIPPEWA SUNS

Stephen Leonard Bjorklund

TATE PUBLISHING
AND ENTERPRISES, LLC

Chippewa Suns
Copyright © 2015 by Stephen Leonard Bjorklund. All rights reserved.

No part of this publication may be reproduced, stored in a retrieval system or transmitted in any way by any means, electronic, mechanical, photocopy, recording or otherwise without the prior permission of the author except as provided by USA copyright law.

This novel is a work of fiction. Names, descriptions, entities, and incidents included in the story are products of the author's imagination. Any resemblance to actual persons, events, and entities is entirely coincidental.

The opinions expressed by the author are not necessarily those of Tate Publishing, LLC.

Published by Tate Publishing & Enterprises, LLC
127 E. Trade Center Terrace | Mustang, Oklahoma 73064 USA
1.888.361.9473 | www.tatepublishing.com

Tate Publishing is committed to excellence in the publishing industry. The company reflects the philosophy established by the founders, based on Psalm 68:11,
"The Lord gave the word and great was the company of those who published it."

Book design copyright © 2015 by Tate Publishing, LLC. All rights reserved.
Cover design by Eileen Cueno
Interior design by Caypeeline Casas

Published in the United States of America
ISBN: 978-1-63418-430-4
Fiction / Native American & Aboriginal
15.05.19

I dedicate this story to the First Nations, to the original inhabitants of the New World. Being rich in culture and history, the Native Americans have contributed as much to mankind as any people, civilization, or nation upon the face of the earth.

Their viability in history can only be measured by facts—they successfully went on about the business of life in this land for ten thousand years. What other civilization can say the same?

 # Contents

	Introduction	9
1	Black Feather	11
2	Gifted Hand	14
3	Two Shadows	17
4	Moon Song, the Word, and the Witch	20
5	Lucky Star	24
6	The True Path	28
7	Myths, Monsters, and Men	31
8	Seasons	36
9	Powwow	40
10	Mountaintop	44
11	The Gift	46
12	Trails	50
13	Shades of Autumn	55
14	Revelation	59
15	Naming	64
16	Death on the Trail: Life in the Word	68
17	Dreamtime	72
18	Something New from Something Old	75
19	Reckoning	92
20	Harvest	96
21	Winds of Change	100
22	Ties That Bind	104
23	The Secret Place	107

24	Spirit Cave	111
25	People and Ideas	116
26	Signs and Wonders	120
27	A Day to Remember	125
28	The Dig	129
29	Saying Good-bye	133
30	Hall of Science	136
31	The Wicker Woman	140
32	In Spirit and Truth	144
33	Kingdoms	149
34	Sweet Air of Home	152
35	The Whirlwind	157

About the Author	161
About the Artist	162
Bibliography and Credits	163

 # INTRODUCTION

AMONG THE NATIVE AMERICANS, THERE is a core belief that life is a great circle, and within this circle lays a cross that touches at four places. These are the four virtues: strength, wisdom, brotherhood, and a true spirit.

America has come to mean freedom to the people of the world. We have been called the light—the flame of the human spirit—but after our arrival in the New World, we committed four sorrows. We took the land from the rightful owners. We mistreated the land. We trafficked in human slavery, and over time, we turned our back upon God.

Many efforts have been made to right these wrongs, and progress has been made at a great price, costing untold thousands the ultimate sacrifice. Yet still, we have not fulfilled our pledge of justice, not in our own eyes, nor in the eyes of God.

Perhaps we should ask the Native American Nations to represent their people in our government and reintroduce the sacred wheel and the four virtues. Perhaps we would find that justice fulfilled can be as powerful a force as freedom.

1

 BLACK FEATHER

"Grandfather, are you sad that I am not a boy so that you could teach me to hunt and fish?"

"Black Feather, come and sit by the fire, and I will tell you the story of the rock and the water, and the tree and the wind."

The young Chippewa maiden sat cross-legged at her grandfather's side, leaned against his legs, letting the glow of the fire dance across her smile, for she knew that the story about to be told by Gifted Hand would warm her to the center of her being.

"At the beginning of things, before the Great Spirit created the people, He made the earth, and the earth was full of wondrous things. There was the green and blue earth itself, and the sky and sunshine and the rain and the snow, and the moon and the starlight. And all of these played upon the face of the land. The Great Spirit observed what He had made, paused, and decided that it was good but that something was missing. So he created all the animals and the birds and everything that moved upon the earth and swam below the waters. He made them male and female so that they would not be alone but would always be a constant friend for each other—mates for life. In this way, there would always and forever be another generation. He paused and observed what he had done and was most pleased."

"But, Grandfather, what about the people?"

Gifted Hand continued, "Yes, the Creator of all there is paused once again and said to himself, 'Who will see my beautiful creation and all my wondrous wildlife? I need to create witnesses, so

I will make people, both men and women, to love and tend all of my creation.'"

"But why, Grandfather, do the people not regard girls and boys in the same way?"

"In the beginning, the rocks were destined to stay upon the ground, silent and in their place and have no voice. So they complained to the Creator, and he made the waters to flow over the rocks, and as they did, a sweet gurgling voice was made to sing and sooth all who would listen. But the trees became jealous, complaining to the Creator that they had no voice, as they were destined to be set in one place upon the earth. So the Creator made the wind, and when it blew upon the outstretched boughs of the trees, it made a most happy sound as it fluttered through the leaves, leaving all who could hear astonished at the loveliness of their voice."

"But, Grandfather, that is all good for the rocks and the water, and the wind and the trees, but what about me? Why can't I have all of the adventures that boys do?"

Gifted Hand added more wood to the campfire. He paused from his story and poked the logs with his fire stick. The wood responded, hissed, and flashed back into life. He began again, "Black Feather, the Great Spirit has created each and every thing with its own purpose, with its own spirit. It is true that boys roam far and wide upon the earth and have many adventures. But they can never give birth to new life. They can never be like the earth itself and nurture that new life. They come, and they go, speaking little, making but a few close friends. Boys are mostly alone with their journeys.

"Girls have all the power of creation within their spirit. They are like the rock and the trees. They occupy the land, they are steady, they make a home. They cherish life and people and make a place worth the living.

"A man roams like the water and the wind. A man can never do or say or think or be the amazing creature that the Great Spirit made women."

The little maiden complained, "What if I want to hunt and fish and go far across the land and have many adventures?"

Gifted Hand replied, "What would the water say without the rock? What would the wind say without the trees? You are my granddaughter, and you will speak life into being. You are the place, the anchor of life, the voice of life. You will have a destiny worthy beyond measure, and I am glad that you're a girl. No man can speak life into being. Now it's time for sleep, and tomorrow you can go with me into the woods and lakes, and I will show you how to hunt and fish. This is an easy thing to teach and a small thing to master. Do you think that you can teach me how to give life?"

"No, Grandfather, I don't think so."

Black Feather watched as Gifted Hand pushed the coals with his fire stick, and she was glad to be who she was, where she was, and with her Grandfather. She knew now that within her was the voice of the people, and she thanked the Great Spirit, then she drifted off into a place of her own, in the land of dreams.

2

 Gifted Hand

The old man moved with the seasons, and many seasons had moved upon him. Now when he paused as he traversed the lake by canoe, bending over the side to trouble the still waters for a handful of refreshment, an old man peered back. *How can this be? I still think the same and feel the same, but my image has drifted somehow to gray... the season of my youth fading in the wake of my passing. I made this birch-bark canoe by my own hand, so, so long ago, the same year Moon Song became my bride. She was then, and remains now, the most amazing creature. I trust all to her—my faithful companion...what a life we share! We have children and grandchildren. We have times of feasting and famine, times of peace, and yes, warfare. Yet through it all she remains my one, true reason.*

His canoe drifted in the still water, his thirst quenched, and once again, he stroked the canoe back into life with his paddle. He only traveled now when he had a mission. The seasons of high adventure—when he had explored the limits of his Chippewa band and when he had helped expand their range by warfare with their enemy the Lakota Sioux—were over. These days, his travels had a simpler purpose: they were duty now to his family, no more youthful intrigues. He would journey to hunt, fish, and gather or to trade with other tribes or with the French and English, who had established frontier posts on the opposite ends of the Chippewa territories.

It was late spring, and his birch bark canoe was heavily laden with furs of beaver and mink, otter and muskrat, and fisher and pine marten. It had been a plentiful fall and winter of trapping, and he also had some bobcat and lynx. He never trapped the wolf or hunted the bears, for they were considered equal as brothers to the Chippewa, their spirits kindred to his own.

Gifted Hand remained a powerful man, both body and spirit, and the seasons had not diminished their enchantment upon his soul. The seasons had left their marks upon his body, however, and a certain amount of pain was also his traveling companion. A tomahawk wound to his left shoulder was a continual reminder of his deadly duel with the infamous Lakota warrior, Screaming Eagle. The Great Spirit had spared Gifted Hand that day and given the powerful enemy unto his hand. Another time, a splendid black bear that he had surprised quite by accident slashed his ribs with a reactionary blow, but his war club found its mark upon the bear's head, ending the unfortunate encounter. His broken ribs had healed, but they still pressed upon his side as he paddled his load of furs.

He preferred trading with the French, for they held a higher opinion of the Chippewa than the English; the French considered the native people as equals. They even intermarried with the Cree tribe, another enemy of the Chippewa. So it was more dangerous for Gifted Hand to enter the French and Cree territory, but he always received the fairest price from the French, so it was worth the risk.

The English were a haughty people to deal with and filled with the pride of self. They did not respect the Chippewa nor did they respect the land, but they were in the home territory controlled by his tribal people. It was safer to trade with the English but not nearly as satisfying.

This trip he had purposed to visit the French traders. He traveled with bow and arrows, his war club, shield, and war lance, but he hoped his journey among the Cree would be peaceful. There had been no clashes with the Cree for nearly a decade, but Gifted Hand remained watchful. His life was not his own—it belonged to his family and his tribe. His safe journey was more important than his own life. He was aware of his greater importance in the service to his tribe. The sale of the furs would mean many essentials: powder, flint, and shot; muskets; seed corn, potatoes, and other garden staples; new steel traps and fine tools such as crosscut saws and axes; and wood chisels and knives. There would also be cast-iron kettles and pans and tin cups and containers.

His tribe had lived for generations without these things, but the Chippewa traveled with the seasons, and now it was the season of the arrival of the strange peoples from across the great waters. It was true that some of their trade goods were a blessing to his people. Even so, Gifted Hand had the presence of mind and spirit to look ahead to a day when his people would pay a greater price for the presence of the foreigners. That season lay far ahead, and he also knew that the people can only occupy one season at a time.

3

 TWO SHADOWS

THE DAY THAT GIFTED HAND had been so badly wounded in battle occurred quite by chance, just as his other wound rendered by the black bear. He had not purposed to go to war that day with his enemy, the Lakota Sioux, just as he had never intended to kill the bear. It was just that in those days, the western territory of the Chippewa overlapped the eastern range of the Sioux. The vast and rich lakes region, of what would become western Minnesota, was a prize highly sought after by both tribes—a contested hunting grounds. That fateful day, deer hunting had inadvertently placed Screaming Eagle and Gifted Hand on a collision course. Screaming Eagle was teaching his only son how to track white tail deer. As the father and son rounded a great boulder, with their focus entirely upon the ground and the tracks of the buck, they came face-to-face with their Chippewa enemy, Gifted Hand. The battle was thrust upon them. Screaming Eagle was a notoriously skilled warrior, and he struck the first blow with his tomahawk. His son had been tracking the deer one step ahead of his father and stumbled and fell against their enemy's legs. In that instant, Screaming Eagle scooped up his son to fling him to safety, and Gifted Hand, reeling in pain, struck back with his war club. The battle was over, a father lay dead, Gifted Hand was gravely wounded, and the boy, Little Eagle, stood alone.

When Gifted Hand returned that day to his encampment, at the foot of the hills that were called "The Seven Sisters," he was not alone. Moon Song was the first to see them.

"What has happened, my husband?"

"We have a new son. His father is dead. He was the great Lakota war chief, Screaming Eagle."

Others from the Chippewa band quickly surrounded the unlikely trio: Little Eagle was taken into Gifted Hand's lodge and fed and cared for; Moon Song and her sister dressed Gifted Hand's shoulder wound, and life went on.

Within weeks, the boy had settled in. He did not hate Gifted Hand—it was not the Indian way—and the boy was immediately accepted by the Chippewa tribe. Gifted Hand knew that every man is the father of every child and that no child is an enemy. They were all of the people. The Great Spirit had made but one tribe; men were the ones to separate themselves in the lost days of long ago, and Little Eagle had a certain standing as the natural son of the great and fearless warrior, Screaming Eagle. Amongst all the tribes and all the peoples, courage was a stronger force than any blood ties. There was only one thing that would never be asked or expected of Little Eagle: he would never be allowed to join a Chippewa war party against his former tribe, the Lakota Sioux. This would be considered a dishonor to the memory of Screaming Eagle and a notion understood by all the people.

Many seasons passed, Little Eagle grew in stature and embraced his place in the tribe, and the day came that he took a bride. Now he was the master of his own lodge and had earned a reputation as a mighty hunter and a wise voice in the tribal council. Gifted Hand was very proud of his adopted son. He had schooled him in the ways of the Chippewa and shared all the wisdom of his people as passed down from generation to generation, going all the way back to the day that the Great Spirit had created the people. Gifted Hand did not neglect to teach Little Eagle about his own tribe, the Lakota Sioux, and about his father, the renowned warrior, Screaming Eagle. In this manner, Little Eagle learned wisdom and the way of the people, for there is but one honorable path through life, and it is called "The Way of the People."

The day came that Little Eagle's wife, "After the Rain," gave birth to a son, and that son would grow tall and straight and strong, and someday would come to be an important person to Gifted Hand's natural granddaughter, Black Feather. He was aptly named "Two Shadows" because he had issued from two extraordinary grandfathers, the one of his blood, Screaming Eagle, and his mentor in life, Gifted Hand. Both of these men had cast a great shadow as they passed upon the Indian lands.

Oftentimes, Two Shadows and Black Feather would sit by the fire and attentively listen to Gifted Hand and Moon Song. The children could never have enough of the presence of their grandparents. Even though Two Shadows was not their grandson by blood, he was in spirit, and Moon Song and Gifted Hand had, by example, demonstrated the bonds of lifelong love to both of the children. Black Feather and Two Shadows had witnessed a place of the heart in the center of Gifted Hands's lodge, and the season of love had also whispered the children's names.

4

Moon Song, the Word, and the Witch

ONE AUSPICIOUS DAY, MOON SONG called Black Feather and Two Shadows and invited them into Gifted Hand's lodge to sit by the fire. Perhaps in some way, she sensed there was something important, even urgent, to share with the children. They loved to hear stories anyway but never had Moon Song told them one before. She began, "Gifted Hand and I love you very much, and we are pleased that you are such caring and respectful children. I must tell you now that there are many forces at work across the Indian nations: some are forces of good, some evil. It may seem a small thing, but what we say and the words that we speak come from our heart, and these words have power, and these words can release the forces of either good or evil. Both of these forces are very real, so think before you speak and try to never hurt other people with your words. Your words should bring life to others and encouragement. Let me share a true story of our tribe. Once there was a beautiful maiden. She was the daughter of two very gifted parents, and they doted upon her and always gave her all manner of precious gifts. The girl became proud and very vain, for her parents had bestowed upon her the finest buckskin garments, with silver and gold and turquoise ornaments and ivory clasps for her hair purchased at great expense from far northern and western tribes. She would sit by the pond for hours and admire her own reflection on the water. One time, her father had been on a raiding party, and some of the enemy were captured, among them a girl of the same age as his own daughter. Her parents brought the captive girl home to their lodge and adopted her so that their own daughter would have a companion to play with. But their real daughter was jealous, not willing to share her parents' affection with any new sister, so she was very cruel to the new girl and said horrible things to her and did mean things to her all the day long. The little girl became so sad and lonely that all the joy of life left her completely, and her heart was broken. Finally, she just wandered away one cold winter day and was never seen or heard from again. So now you see what words can accomplish—life or death!" Moon Song looked at the attentive children and asked, "Will you always remember what I have said to you?"

Both children promised even though they had not entirely understood the gravity of the message, and then they shared sweet potato cakes and hot cornmeal mush covered with maple syrup. This time with Moon Song was lodged in their memories as a most mysterious but enjoyable afternoon. They wondered who the proud maiden of their tribe was.

As their time with Moon Song ended, they walked out of Gifted Hand's lodge. Two Shadows asked Black Feather as they walked side by side, "Did you understand all that she said?"

Before Black Feather could respond, many horses and people entered the village from the west, and there was a great commotion. Some of the young braves had led a raiding party against the Lakota and had captured six horses and one Sioux maiden.

"Let's go and see," said Black Feather.

There was much shouting and boasting and war whooping by the returning braves, as they were filled up with the displays of their successful raid and filled up with themselves as well. Everyone in the village came out of their lodges and encircled the braves, even Owl Woman, the old witch. People made a wide space around Owl Woman; no one wanted to stand next to her or even very close to her. In point of fact, most of the people in the tribe did not even want Owl Woman to look upon them.

It was the custom of the tribe that trophies of war could be kept or sold to the highest bidder. The five bigger horses went quickly, and the braves parlayed their prize into muskets and furs and lodge poles for their future tepees. When the last horse, a small paint, was put up for trade, Owl Woman stepped forward. "I will offer a spirit bag of good fortune to the lucky brave that gives me the painted horse."

Someone from the back of the crowd, who Owl Woman could not see, shouted out, "What would an old woman do with a horse?"

The crowd quieted, and even the victorious braves of the raiding party backed away from Owl Woman. She finally croaked a response in her gravelly voice, saying, "The winters are long, and few of you leave me any food. I know each of you, and I keep track of who gives me venison or smoked fish and also who gives me nothing. A fine young horse will be good meat for me in the last months of winter."

"Bite your tongue then, you old hag. That should last you for the rest of the winter," said another unseen voice from the back of the crowd. The whole village reeled at the comment and backed farther away from the old woman's wrath.

She glared at the back of the crowd, turned, and said through her blackened and broken teeth, "And while you're at it, sell me the Sioux maiden. I could use her as my slave. There is much work undone at my lodge."

Moon Song stepped forward and confronted Owl Woman: "I will make sure that the work is done at your lodge and that you have enough to eat this winter, but you shall not have this young girl—now be gone from this assembly."

The crowd gasped and was astonished at the courage and boldness of Moon Song. Owl Woman's eyes flashed with hatred, like a thunderclap and lightning, and she hissed at Moon Song, then at the crowd, "We shall see what we shall see." Then she whisked herself away down the hillside and disappeared into the blackness of her lodge.

Moon Song turned to the braves and bartered for the horse and the Sioux maiden. The braves were glad to conclude this business and to quickly put an end to the dark encounter with Owl Woman.

Moon Song went to the captive maiden and said, "You are free to live with me and Gifted Hand and take your place in our lodge, or you are free to leave with the paint."

The young maiden rushed forward and hugged Moon Song and tearfully kissed her hands, but she was so frightened by the Owl Woman that she immediately left with the paint to rejoin her people.

After that day, the children would come to know that Moon Song's words were true. Moon Song faithfully kept her spoken pledge, and twice each week, she went to Owl Woman's lodge and did the chores. And with the onset of winter, Moon Song made certain that the old woman always had enough to eat. Owl Woman should have been grateful, but instead, she plotted against Moon Song. When spring came, she journeyed far to the western edge of the Chippewa territory and tried to bribe some Lakota braves with silver, gold, turquoise, and ivory, into kidnapping Moon Song. She told them all of the hideous things that they should do to Moon Song to satisfy her own lust for revenge. Instead, the Sioux warriors did all these same things to Owl Woman and sent back her charred and broken bones in a leather sack to her Chippewa tribe, with a pictographic warning on the buckskin to send them no more witches.

Black Feather and Two Shadows heard of the tale, and now they truly understood about the power of words. They had come to realize that the Owl Woman had once been the beautiful maiden of Moon Song's story. Owl Woman's lifetime of wicked words had even had a way of distorting and disfiguring her own youthful beauty, and in the end, her words also became her own death sentence.

5

 ## Lucky Star

THE DEATH OF THE OLD witch, Owl Woman, was a lifting of a great burden from the Chippewa. Everyone had been obliged to tolerate her wicked presence because the people would never banish or harm one of their own—it was not their way. Thankfully, at times, the Great Spirit had a way of sorting out events and people.

Two Shadows, however, had another source of uneasiness. Within his spirit, he was unsettled with his past. His grandfather had been the mighty Lakota war chief, Screaming Eagle, and an archenemy of the Chippewa. Two Shadows's father, Little Eagle, had been orphaned and then adopted by the Chippewa band. The boy always wondered about the Lakota Sioux, and because he also had within him the courage of his forefathers, he decided to journey west and seek out the people of his ancestors. He knew that this desire might result in much danger, for the Lakota were the sworn enemy of his present-day tribe, the Chippewa, and that they might kill him on sight before even one word could pass between them.

He asked permission to borrow a horse from his father, Little Eagle, and he also asked for a blessing from his adoptive grandfather, Gifted Hand. Both of these tribal leaders understood that the boy was about to venture out upon his first spirit quest, and they commenced to bless him and then release him to the Great Spirit. Both men knew they might never see Two Shadows again. The way of the people taught that all men must seek and find the path of a true human being, and no one else could walk this path for Two Shadows.

He left one sunny morning, his mind and spirit irrepressible and intent upon a far horizon. Black Feather watched as he disappeared from view, tears appearing and leaving the trace of love upon her face. It was little over one hard day's journey on horseback from Two Shadows's encampment by the hills of the Seven Sisters to the stronghold of the Lakota Sioux at the beginning of the Great Plains. The landscape changed abruptly from the hills and the woods and the lakes to the flats, the tall grass prairies, and the kingdom ruled over by the buffalo and the fearsome plains warriors, the Lakota.

Late the following day, in the heat of the afternoon, Two Shadows spotted a small paint horse. He recognized this animal. He had seen it the day that the Chippewa braves of his band had returned with horses and the Sioux maiden. Two Shadows warily approached. The horse was tethered to a cottonwood tree, and beyond the tree, there was a small, round pond. There was a girl swimming alone and naked.

Two Shadows did not want to frighten her, so he turned his back to the pond and called out, "Maiden of the pond, what is your name? This is Two Shadows speaking to you, grandson of Screaming Eagle."

The girl swiftly swam to shore and hastily dressed again in her buckskins, struggling to pull on her knee-high moccasins over wet feet. She said as she dressed, "How is it that you claim to be the grandson of Screaming Eagle? He was of my tribe, and I have never even heard your name."

"I will tell you my story if you will tell me your name and take me to your people," Two Shadows boldly announced.

"I am called Lucky Star. Tell me your story then…and perhaps the rest can follow."

The two young people sat in the shadow of the great cottonwood next to their horses, with the late evening sun reflecting red and lavender upon the mirrored face of the maiden's swimming hole. When Two Shadows was done recounting his tale, Lucky Star proclaimed, "I know your people. I was the girl that Moon Song saved from the old witch…and I will take you to my people! Ride close to me, and say nothing when we reach the outriders of my village. I must convince them quickly that you are truly the grandson of Screaming Eagle, or they will surely strike you down."

Two Shadows, thanks to the entreaties of Lucky Star, made it past the warrior sentries and was received by the elders of the tribe. Many still living had known and ridden with the war chief, Screaming Eagle.

After a hearty welcome and a bountiful meal, Two Shadows attended a special tribal council held especially in his honor. The head elder, Buffalo Thunder, told Two Shadows the story of his Lakota Tribe and of the great feats of his best friend, Screaming Eagle. They ended the nightlong event with the story about Gifted Hand, their Chippewa enemy. Buffalo Thunder spoke, "The loss of Screaming Eagle was a shocking blow to our people. We had gathered quickly together to war against the Chippewa band that camped at the foot of the hills at Seven Sisters. I was the lead scout, and as I approached the place where Screaming Eagle and Gifted Hand had warred upon each other, I spotted smoke coming up from a small fire. Gifted Hand was kneeling down and fanning the smoke up and away and over the burial platform that he had built with his own hands for Screaming Eagle. He had carefully laid his enemy to rest atop the raised platform, with all of Screaming Eagle's weapons arranged according to our custom. He had covered Screaming Eagle with his own best ceremonial buffalo robe, and he was singing prayer songs to honor his fallen enemy.

"I returned to the war party, and we broke off the planned attack. Gifted Hand had proven himself a most worthy and honorable adversary, earning the respect of our tribe—and a truce."

Two Shadows remained at the Lakota village for several more days, meeting all his uncles and aunts and cousins. At the end of the week, the Sioux were obliged to depart many days to the west; it was the season to follow and hunt the buffalo, and it was understood by all that it was time for the visitor to return to his people, to the Seven Sisters Chippewa encampment. Lucky Star rode with him as far as her swimming hole. They dismounted briefly next to the cottonwood tree, and she hugged him long and hard. No words were passed, and Two Shadows and Lucky Star remounted their horses, each to embark upon their separate journeys. The Great Spirit indeed had a way of sorting out events and people.

6

 ## The True Path

BLACK FEATHER SANG MANY SONGS for Two Shadows as he undertook his dangerous mission. She prayed to the Great Spirit, the one true God, the Creator of all there is, for his safe return. The entire village was anxious, especially Two Shadows's parents and grandparents. Each had placed their petitions before the Great Spirit.

Prayers answered, he finally returned to the Seven Sisters village, and a spontaneous and joyful celebration broke out. The people donned their finest attire and held a day of feasting. It was expected of Two Shadows to share the fruits of his spirit quest and reveal everything about his adventure with the Lakota Sioux, leaving no detail untold. Black Feather doted upon each word but was more than a little anxious when Two Shadows recounted his meeting with the Sioux maiden, Lucky Star, but she had the good sense not to press him on the matter. She knew the power of words, thanks to Moon Song's teachings. The season of love sometimes required the seasoning of patience.

Gifted Hand had also been moved by the young man's narrative. He had never known that the Lakota warrior, Buffalo Thunder, had silently observed him that day—the day that he had honored Screaming Eagle. Gifted Hand wondered about the truce that Buffalo Thunder had spoken of and whether that good will could possibly lead to a final cessation of hostilities between their warring tribes, a lasting peace. He hoped so. He also wondered if Two Shadows might serve as an acceptable go-between for their tribes, by virtue of his connection to both.

The seasons spun round and round, and now it was early fall and time for the young to learn the skills of the hunt. Their Chippewa band was superbly positioned at the base of the Seven Sisters Hills and also adjacent to Spirit Lake where each fall thousands of ducks and geese would congregate. Gifted Hand began the lessons, showing his grandchildren how to prepare for the hunt, first to gather materials from nature's storehouse to fashion duck decoys, then the plan of how to place the decoys and arrange their blind on the shore of Spirit Lake, but most importantly, how to hold a ceremony to thank the Great Spirit for the bounty of the gift of the waterfowl. The Chippewa were a spiritual people and, in all good things, gave thanks to the Creator. They started a small fire next to their blind and fanned the smoke over their faces, then toward the lake to honor their most handsome quarry—the red and scarlet headed ducks with the white sides and backs.

These ducks were so agile in the air that Gifted Hand instructed the children to wait until they landed amongst the decoys and then to take careful aim with their bow and arrows as the ducks floated still upon the waters.

Two Shadows focused upon the newly made decoys and marveled at how real they appeared. They had been fashioned of tightly wound bulrush leaves covered with white birch bark and made in four parts, stitched smoothly together with willow whips, and dyed with red and black berries. They were held in place by rawhide buckskin cording, fastened to small bits of musket bar lead. They bobbed and swirled in the breeze just like real live ducks.

Black Feather observed as the canvasback and redhead ducks began to mill about over the lake, seeing that their flight was truly a wondrous thing. They rose and fell with the wind, a single creature formed of many parts, a cloud of ducks with one mind, one will. They moved in perfect rhythm and tempo as a glorious song of fall, each knowing his or her part and proper place within the fluid harmony of the flock. In this movement, the Great Spirit revealed his voice. Black Feather was deeply touched by what she was witnessing.

Seven canvasbacks landed in the decoys. Gifted Hand gave a nod to the children to take aim and make their shot. Two Shadows found his target, a large bull canvasback, and released his arrow. The impact, splash, and commotion caused the other ducks to take flight before Black Feather could loose her arrow.

"Go fetch your duck!" Gifted Hand said jubilantly.

The boy waded out to the decoy spread and retrieved his four-pound prize. He brought the canvasback to Black Feather, and he laid it in her lap. The male duck was the most beautiful creature she had ever seen. Its eyes were open, and a drop of water slid down below its eye, like a tear. With the perfection that rested upon her lap, she knew that her aspiration to become a hunter, to travel far, and have all of the adventures that boys have was over. She would learn to prepare the ducks and other wild bounty for meals for her people but never would she take a life. Within her gentle spirit, Black Feather had found her own kind of peace, her own path as a true human being.

Two Shadows, however, had fired the first arrow of a lifetime of insuring food and safety for his people and to becoming a steadfast provider for his future bride.

7

 ## MYTHS, MONSTERS, AND MEN

BUFFALO THUNDER, WAR CHIEF OF the Lakota Sioux, had thought long and hard about his experience with his sworn enemy, Gifted Hand. He had also considered his best friend, Screaming Eagle, who had died at the hands of this Chippewa. And then there was the boy, Two Shadows, whose parents were of both tribes.

There had been nearly thirty years of warfare between their tribes, and it seemed right to him for the bad blood to end. He decided to summon Two Shadows. He would prepare a peace belt, as a sign to his enemy, and make entreaties through the boy to Gifted Hand. But how was he to contact the Chippewa without inciting a confrontation? Not one of the rival tribes was safe entering the other's territory. Instant combat and death awaited any brave who would dare to trespass. Also, it was not the Indian way to bluntly state their business; this, too, would be considered a provocation and unforgiveable lapse of protocol between the tribes. So how was Buffalo Thunder to arrange an invitation? A notion came into his mind.

On a recent buffalo hunt to the western prairie, he had stumbled upon a most remarkable find. The prairie winds and rain had unearthed the skull of a monstrous beast. No one of his tribe had ever seen anything so terrible. Curiosity was a universal human force, and perhaps the mystery of the beast could serve as an excuse to invite a respected elder of an enemy tribe for a temporary truce to investigate this great oddity. Both the Lakota Sioux and the Chippewa were fascinated with all aspects of creation. Buffalo Thunder decided to enlist Lucky Star to go to the Seven Sisters Chippewa band and ask her new friend, Two Shadows, for a visit. Without hesitation, she agreed.

Moon Song was the first to see the paint horse cresting the highest peak of the Seven Sisters Hills. She hurried to meet Lucky Star to insure her safe passage into the village.

When Lucky Star recognized Moon Song, she immediately dismounted and hastened to meet her. She gave Moon Song a heartfelt hug and said, "We finally meet again. I think of you often and remember how you saved me from the witch."

Moon Song replied, "I am so glad that you are well. I, too, think of you every day. You have blossomed into such a beautiful young woman. What brings you to our village?"

"I have been entrusted by our tribal elder, Buffalo Thunder, to invite Two Shadows to our camp. I believe that Buffalo Thunder wishes to open talks between our two tribes."

"Let's go and find Gifted Hand, and you can explain your mission. I will stay at your side, so do not be afraid, and you can lodge with us and be our honored guest."

When Moon Song found Gifted Hand, he was busy showing Black Feather and Two Shadows how to trap fish. They were installing a willow branch fish weir at the mouth of a stream by Spirit Lake. Two Shadows jumped to his feet and greeted Lucky Star and introduced her to Gifted Hand and Black Feather. The young ladies studied each other for the longest time. Much was said without a word being passed. Moon Song ended the awkward moment and said, "This young lady has been sent by Buffalo Thunder to ask your permission for Two Shadows to visit their village."

Gifted Hand smiled and replied, "I have thought of Buffalo Thunder many times, and I welcome this invitation. Two Shadows, are you willing to journey to the Lakota Sioux encampment?"

"I am, Grandfather."

"Then let us pause now and share a meal in our lodge. You young people can depart tomorrow at first light," said Gifted Hand.

Once more, Black Feather had to release Two Shadows to the Great Spirit. This time, the hazard was a challenge to the affairs of the heart. The next morning, the Sioux maiden led Black Feather's true love away to a distant and uncertain horizon.

Buffalo Thunder greeted the returning children, and formalities were exchanged. At the evening meal that night, Buffalo Thunder laid the matter before him. "We have a mystery to solve. We have found the remains of a great beast far to the west on the Buffalo Prairie. This is such an alarming sight that I wish to pose a truce with your grandfather, Gifted Hand, so that we may journey together and see this great wonder and find the meaning of the creature."

"When do you want him to come?" Two Shadows inquired.

"Before the season of snow."

"I shall carry your message at once," said Two Shadows, and he immediately set out to rejoin his tribe.

Gifted Hand received the invitation with gladness. Perhaps peace could be found on the Buffalo Prairie. Moon Song had also informed her husband of Black Feather's anxiety and counseled him to take both Two Shadows and Black Feather along on this most important journey. Gifted Hand had learned to honor Moon Song's requests.

Within this same momentous week, the trio had reached the Lakota Sioux encampment, and Gifted Hand was welcomed as a powerful and honored adversary. That evening there was feasting and introductions. At sunrise, the two former enemies and the three youngsters, Black Feather, Lucky Star, and Two Shadows set out for the western prairie and their appointment with destiny. They finally arrived at the location of the great skull and set up camp.

It was well after sundown as the group finished building a big fire. The children walked to the skull of the beast, and they stood staring at the immense jaws and the spear-like rows of teeth. The skull was as big as Lucky Star's paint horse, and the reflected light from the campfire animated the huge, ghostly eyes and the hideous smile of the beast.

"Come away and back by the fire, children," ordered Buffalo Thunder.

Buffalo Thunder looked at Gifted Hand and asked, "What do you think of this monstrous beast?"

Gifted Hand poked the fire with a stick and said, "I have never even heard of the existence of such a creature, not even in all of the ancient legends of my people."

Buffalo Thunder motioned to the youngsters to gather closer to him and Gifted Hand, and then he began to tell a story: "Once, long ago when I was but a boy, like Two Shadows, my father took me along to sell some furs at the French trading post in the far north. While there, we met a man who claimed he was a Jesuit priest from a land far across the great waters, a land called Spain. I don't remember how the subject arose, but the priest told of a most strange tale, one that I share with you now. He said, 'There was a great battle in heaven before the Creator had placed men upon this earth. Two-thirds of the heavenly angels remained loyal to the one true God, but one-third of the angels rebelled against Him, and there was war in heaven. The evil angels were defeated and cast out of heaven and down upon the earth. Some took the forms of monsters and demon beasts. The monsters eventually all died off before men walked the earth, but their wicked spirits still inhabit the land.' And that was the end of the priest's account. The creature that we have journeyed together to see, here on the Buffalo Prairie, may be proof that the priest from Spain spoke truly."

The two men and the children just watched the flames of the campfire reflect upon the skull of the beast, but no more was said on that account.

The next morning, Buffalo Thunder went to his pack horse and retrieved the peace belt, a white piece of buckskin adorned with beads and tassels of braided horse hair imbedded with turquoise. He took Gifted Hand by the forearm, and Gifted Hand grasped his old enemy's forearm, and the peace belt was passed between them.

"There is much to work out between our peoples," said Buffalo Thunder.

"Then let us begin," said Gifted Hand.

The group then departed, Gifted Hand proudly bearing the peace belt home to his people. Black Feather was relieved at the prospect for peace, but only time could tell about a more personal journey, the direction of Two Shadows's heart.

8

 ## Seasons

One overcast day, the snow began to fall upon the Seven Sisters Chippewa encampment and continued for three days. This was the first snow of many that would remain until spring. Each member of the tribe, young and old, was continuing preparations for the long winter ahead. The ice became strong enough, and the braves began to set up dark house tepees upon the north bay of Spirit Lake. Here they could spear the northern pike, walleye, and largemouth bass, which would help to sustain the people over the lean times ahead.

All fall, the people had gathered bundles of hay grass as fodder for their horses, and the women were now occupied with sorting and storing corn, wild rice, potatoes and sweet potatoes, carrots, squash, and pumpkins. Everything was set aside and protected in the proper way and in the proper place. As the men brought in their day's catch from the lake, the women set the fish upon smoking racks and tended the fires so that the fish were cured and preserved to perfection.

Now that there was ice on the ponds, the men and boys began their winter trap lines. The lakes provided mink, otter, muskrat, and beaver. In the fields and forests, fox, coyotes, fishers, pine martens, ermine, raccoon, bobcat, and lynx were the prize. Rabbits, grouse, and wild turkey were snared by the women for food. The women also stretched and scraped the hides, making them suitable for clothing, bedding, tepee sidewalls, and, most importantly, for trade with the French and English. Only buffalo hides were never traded. These were a sacred gift from the Great Spirit meant only for The People.

The men began to hunt in earnest for deer, elk, and, on the southwestern plains below the heavy snowline, buffalo. Many of the braves banded together for safety on these hunts. It was wiser for a larger group to go after this most prized and dangerous quarry. A bull buffalo, when pressed or wounded, would turn on a mounted brave, and in years gone by, many Chippewa had been killed or seriously wounded. In fact, Black Feather's Father had died in such a manner, shortly after pneumonia had taken her Mother. From that day on, Moon Song and Gifted Hand became both her parents and grandparents.

Many braves hunting close together could head off or kill, with many well-aimed spears, a charging bull. Another danger also attended these hunts. The Chippewa would be encroaching upon the grounds of the Lakota Sioux and their ally, the Cheyenne. If discovered, warfare became a likely and deadly possibility. The People needed the buffalo to survive the winter, so the risks were necessary for them all.

The men and women of The People held a very different concept of life and death. The women were creatures of relationship: they embraced life and dreaded the loss of one of their own. To them, there was no glory in loss—only pain and sorrow. The men, however, saw death as part of the circle of life, just another season. They were willing to lay down their life every day. Their path was all about duty, and the value of a man was not measured in the length of his years but the depth of his personal honor and courage. In a way, the continual warring with neighboring tribes afforded them the medium upon which they could demonstrate their bravery. Long or short was of no importance—a brave life was the much sought after prize. That is why a lasting peace between the tribes was so elusive. Warring was a necessary element in this manly contest. This fact was a considerable source of frustration to the Indian women, and they universally hated war and the loss of their loved ones and detested all the foolish boasting and posturing of men. There existed one fateful irony, however, one naked fact. No young maiden desired a husband who had not proven his courage. Given a choice, the bravest of the braves ended up with the most desirable maidens. Peace became the casualty of the affairs of men.

As the tribes, the Chippewa and the Lakota Sioux, entered into the depths of winter, these things played upon the spirits of the two tribal elders: both Buffalo Thunder and Gifted Hand were obliged to seek a new path for their people. Old hatreds, overlapping territories, contested hunting grounds, and the pride of men would all be obstacles in the way of this peace. But the warriors and one-time enemies would gladly trade their own lives to see this peace at last, and they both pressed forward to find the way. Both old men began to accompany every Buffalo hunt that winter, a burdensome challenge to their aging bodies, and several times, they did encounter their enemy on the southwestern plains on the Buffalo wintering grounds. The old men saw to it that no warfare ensued. When they met, the old war leaders halted their braves, raised a hand of peace, and both groups gave space to one another. They remained in sight of each other but did not hunt together. It was a fragile truce—but indeed a new beginning.

By the end of winter and with the onset of spring, a few of the Lakota Sioux began to venture into Chippewa territory to hunt deer or spear fish at the mouth of the creeks by Spirit Lake. The Chippewa warriors kept track of their movements but allowed them to go about their hunting and gathering unmolested. No brave wanted the dishonor of breaking the truce or in provoking their old enemy.

Gifted Hand was so pleased by the behavior of both tribes that he decided to send Two Shadows to the Lakota Sioux and present an invitation to Buffalo Thunder and his fellow tribal elders to come for a powwow at the Seven Sisters village.

"Grandfather," inquired Two Shadows, "may I invite some of the young Lakota to come also? We could share some games, and maybe I could get to know my cousins."

"Would you also invite Lucky Star?"

"Of course, if you insist, Grandfather."

"Don't forget Black Feather in your schemes… We wouldn't want to restart the war," laughed Gifted Hand.

So that spring, for the first time in over thirty years, the Chippewa people and the Lakota Sioux met by the shores of Spirit Lake to celebrate a winter without warfare and the possible spring of a lasting peace. And three young people, Black Feather, Lucky Star, and Two Shadows, would come together once again and see how the Great Spirit would sift their hearts and sort out their futures.

9

Powwow

TIME WAS A LIVING THING to the Indian peoples; it had shape and form and texture, and you could track it through the people's lives as you could track a deer in fresh snow. Time left a mark upon them all, its face ever changing as the seasons; but also, like seasons, it moved as the great circle of life. When a season of time had run its course, you just knew that it would return again, and you learned to move in harmony with the season at hand. War and peace were seasons as well, and now, finally, after many long winters of war, peace was again calling to The People.

Everyone was truly exuberant about the coming powwow, and to a person, they all knew that history was being made as the Lakota Sioux began to arrive at the Seven Sisters Chippewa stronghold. Former enemies looked upon each other face-to-face, barely able to control their excitement and curiosity. Everyone was dressed in their finest regalia, and the warrior chiefs of both tribes were a sight to behold with their tasseled buckskins, beaded moccasins, eagle-feathered headdress and feathered trains, porcupine-ribbed breastplate, and colorful war shields and war clubs dangling at their sides—what a picture of nobility. The women and maidens were stunning as well, with their long and shining black hair adorned with ivory, turquoise, and golden clips and their buckskins studded with precious metals, seashells, and gemstones.

All the Lakota guests brought gifts and articles to trade and gamble. Many magnificent horses were also brought for trade and for games of skill. It was truly going to be an event to remember for all ages to come. The thirty years of warfare had been a dark time, but now they walked in light. There was a great release of the spirit in this powwow, and all in attendance could sense the presence of the Great Spirit among them.

Buffalo Thunder carried his tribe's impressive peace pipe, cradled across his folded arms, a sacred instrument made from the finest hardwood, with a tobacco bowl of precious pipestone. He was welcomed by Gifted Hand, also adorned in his finest ceremonial garments, with the white buckskin peace belt draped across his folded arms.

The day began with introductions, and it was soon apparent that Two Shadows had invited the entire Lakota Sioux tribe. There were even toddlers and infants in the cradle packs carried by their mothers. The guests quickly settled in and were led to the center of the village where the Chippewa women had laid out a great banquet. The entire group broke up into smaller circles: men with men, women with women, young braves with young braves, and maidens with maidens. They talked and ate and laughed, shared stories, and did it all over again until they could eat and drink no more.

After a while with the group, Black Feather and Lucky Star moved apart and sat side by side, the young ladies truly enjoying each other's company. Black Feather finally asked what they both needed to know, "What are you and I to do about Two Shadows?"

Lucky Star reached out and took both of Black Feather's hands in her own and said, "We both have love for him, and this love is true. We can never be ashamed of love. I am willing, if you are willing, to let the Great Spirit lead us in this."

Black Feather was truly touched by the tender heart and wisdom, of Lucky Star. She finally replied, "In the end, the choice must be Two Shadows's. I will never think badly or speak badly of you."

Lucky Star answered, "Then let us both freely follow our hearts and wait and see." The two young ladies had made their own kind of peace, and from that day forward, no matter the outcome, they would remain as sisters.

The powwow lasted three days and nights, and the young braves played games of skill, rough and tumble games with a leather ball and curved clubs, and goalposts. This game was just short of warfare, and many impressive bruises decorated the ablest players. There was a horse riding exhibition, with bow and arrows and war lances and targets of squash and pumpkins. The men traded for horses and gambled for trade goods such as steel tomahawks and long belt knives. It was a glorious time for all.

The tribal elders, led by Gifted Hand and Buffalo Thunder, established guidelines to control hunting, fishing, and gathering and trapping in each other's territory. They also discussed, but did not formally agree, on a mutual defense pact if they were attacked by other tribes. They also discussed the possibility of future conflict with the ever-increasing numbers of French and English, but nothing was decided. Future events would dictate further talks. It was agreed that the encroachment of the foreigners bore watching.

The last night after sundown, all gathered in the center of the village. The elders from both tribes sat around two giant drums, big as the floor inside a tepee, and they sang and chanted and beat upon on the drums until well into the night. The young braves and the maidens danced around a great bonfire, their tassels and feathers and leather tunics flying in the air. They had bells upon their leggings, and each time they stomped the earth, they sounded in perfect time with the beat of the drums. Such a spectacular powwow had never been seen before and might never be seen again.

The next morning, the guests departed, former things had passed away, and now a new thing. Lucky Star and Black Feather also embraced and parted with a smile. Two Shadows witnessed the exchange and was slightly mystified, but he quickly regained himself and said a rousing good-bye to his cousins. Everyone stopped and watched as Gifted Hand and Buffalo Thunder took leave of each other. The peace pipe had been passed, the peace belt honored, and the old adversaries were free at last to see their dream fulfilled.

10

Mountaintop

"My life is one long thought interrupted only by actions. Even in sleep, this thought continues," said Two Shadows.

He lay on the grassy top of the Seven Sisters Hills, his hands clasped behind his head like a pillow. Black Feather lay next to him the same. They had slipped away from the village to gain the best vantage point to see the stars. It was a perfectly black night, midsummer hot, and the heavens were as bright as they could ever be. Soon the young people would be treated to a celestial gift. A once-in-a-lifetime happening.

"Sometimes, I imagine that everything exists in the mind of the Great Spirit, and if he lost that thought, we would all fall from the sky like a shooting star," responded Black Feather.

"Are we our own or an extension of our parents and grandparents? Does anything change, or are we just different seasons in the same lifetime?" Two Shadows posed.

Just then, the meteor shower began, and they both stopped speaking, stopped thinking, and became witness to a heavenly display like no other. The Great Spirit was speaking to them both, and his thoughts were radiant. They were overwhelmed. The shooting stars replaced all their ponderings but one. On the mountaintop, they lay together under the streaking starlight side by side in the sweet clover, completely in love.

As the shooting stars illuminated the sky overhead, the crickets began to sing like there would be no tomorrow. Two Shadows gently slid his arm under Black Feather, and she placed her head upon his shoulder and her hand upon his chest. His heart was beating in perfect time with the orchestrated crescendos of the crickets. She could feel his heart in her hand. She wished upon the shooting stars to hold onto this hour forever.

A wolf began to sing out and was soon joined by the rest of his pack. They were spread out and stationed on the hills to the west and were marking their location to each other by their songs. Soon a deer hunt would commence, and Two Shadows knew it was time for the young couple to return to the Seven Sisters village.

11
The Gift

Along the way, something had happened to the young people. You cannot capture time, and Black Feather, Two Shadows, and Lucky Star were compelled by the passing seasons to journey onward. The things of childhood had slipped away, except in their spirit where one thing would always remain: the joy of shared memories.

Two Shadows had struggled with the reality of his life: he was by blood of two tribes, two peoples, and in his heart, he had truly loved two enchanting maidens. There was no choosing between Black Feather and Lucky Star, but he must choose. It would soon be the season to take a bride, that is, after he had proven himself worthy. He must first perform some great and noble deed, risk everything, and earn his place among the warrior braves of his band. Only in this way could he earn the right to ask one of the maidens to be his for life. Two Shadows began to seek the will of the Great Spirit in earnest, and he frequently separated himself from everyone to go into the sweat lodge to be purified and to seek a vision. He prayed earnestly for the Great Spirit to show him the way.

Two Shadows had become a complicated man, a thinking man. He shared one rock-solid connection to every true warrior who had ever walked upon this earth, he had no fear of death, but he harbored a deathly fear of dishonor. His sense of duty to his people filled every sinew of his being. But he had seen the other side of courage: the wisdom of the people. Both men whom he respected the most, the men he truly longed to be like, had moved past war and reached with all their being for peace. The war chiefs, Gifted Hand and Buffalo Thunder, had shown him a different path—one that embraced life and lifted up all the people as worthy. How then was he ever going to prove himself? His world had changed in such a way that there were no easy answers. Perhaps a simple, uncluttered, unthinking mind was best. If you are born of warriors, be a warrior. If you are born of lesser men, then smaller ambitions might suffice. This would never do for Two Shadows. The blood of warrior chiefs cried out from his veins—just as the love of two women warred upon his heart.

Moon Song came unexpectedly one morning to the sweat lodge where Two Shadows had been continually seeking answers to his struggles. She said softly, "I am sorry to disturb you, but you have a visitor."

He exited the sweat lodge, nearly naked except for a loincloth, and poured cold water over his head and body from an earthen ware jug next to the lodge, set there for that purpose. He quickly dried himself and pulled on his buckskins. Lucky Star was standing alongside Moon Song, and she looked away as he dressed.

She finally said, "I have a gift for you and for Black Feather. Please accept this yellow wolf-dog as my blessing upon you both."

"What does this mean?"

"My father has promised me to another brave, a Cheyenne warrior. It was a move on his part to help strengthen the pact and the resolve between our two tribes. We are engaged in a great struggle with our enemy to the west, the Pawnee, and this marriage will help our people to survive. The Cheyenne brave is the son of their chief, as I am the daughter of our chief. The Pawnee are a powerful and fearsome enemy—without mercy—and only by joining with the Cheyenne can we hope to avoid destruction. I am so sorry."

Two Shadows kneeled down and embraced the dog, and the wolf-sized animal licked his face and wagged his tail with such gusto that his entire torso moved. "What's his name?"

"I've called him Star. In this name, part of me will be with you always. Please greet Black Feather for me. I have no time. I must return to my people immediately. We are expecting another attack by the Pawnee."

Without any hesitation, Two Shadows said to Moon Song, "Take Star to Black Feather and tell her what has happened. I am going with Lucky Star to help defend her people. I must gather my weapons and ready my horse at once."

The Great Spirit was moving upon the lives of Two Shadows, Lucky Star, and Black Feather with events of a most startling magnitude and an even more uncertain outcome.

Lucky Star rode swiftly on her paint horse with the young brave at her side. They arrived at the Lakota Sioux encampment just in time for the young man to join in a council of war. Sioux scouts had detected a very large Pawnee war party approaching from the Buffalo Prairie. The Lakota plan of attack was quickly devised. Two Shadows and his cousins would join the young braves and charge into the approaching Pawnees, fire three arrows each, and then retreat across the flats to the high ground by Buffalo Butte. The main force of the Lakota Sioux and their Cheyenne allies would be waiting atop the butte on three sides of the valley, ready to swoop down upon the enemy. If the ruse was successful, the young Lakota braves would appear as a raiding party caught unawares by the massed Pawnee warriors. They were the bait for a trap, a most risky gamble indeed.

Two Shadows played his part and, in this first ever combat, distinguished himself as a fearless warrior. The young braves did indeed strike at the center of the Pawnee war party and charged into a cloud of hissing arrows. Two Shadows was at the head of the Lakota and was struck twice, once in the leg, once in the shoulder. He couldn't draw his bow, so he pressed in close to the enemy and attacked with his war club, striking down three Pawnee warriors. The young braves followed the war plan and retreated to Buffalo Butte, leading the enraged Pawnee toward the hidden Sioux and Cheyenne. Three of Two Shadows's cousins lay dead, and nearly every one of the braves had been wounded. All horses were struck by at least one arrow, but the war ponies to a horse returned their riders to safety, and the gamble had gone their way this day.

The ensuing battle was the largest in the memory of the men now living, and the losses on both sides were horrendous. There was one indisputable outcome, the Lakota Sioux and their Cheyenne allies had carried the day, and the Pawnee had been dealt a crippling blow from which it would take their tribe an entire generation to recover.

Both Buffalo Thunder and Two Shadows had paid a price for this victory, each had been severely wounded, but with time, both would recover.

It was three months before Two Shadows was fit enough to ride to the Seven Sisters village, but once again, the Great Spirit had sifted hearts and sorted events. The Creator of all there is had provided a path no one could have ever foreseen. Two Shadows's heart was free; Lucky Star had set him free. He had kept faith with all that he loved and kept the peace of Buffalo Thunder and Gifted Hand. He had demonstrated to himself that he was worthy of his true love. He had faced his fear and found his personal honor.

After greetings all around, he approached Black Feather and said, "There needs to be words between us. Let's take the yellow dog and go to the mountaintop."

Gifted Hand and Moon Song watched as the ones they loved the most journeyed hand in hand to the top of the highest hill, escorted by the most worthy of gifts, a wolf-dog named Star.

12

Trails

It was decided. The season of weddings was in the winds. Black Feather and Two Shadows had become engaged at their secret place atop the highest hill of the Seven Sisters. They would wed in the spring. News had also come to them that Lucky Star and her Cheyenne brave, Dusty Swan, would wed the fall of the same year.

Two Shadows had always dreamed of seeing the great lake of Chippewa legend, Gitche Gumee, and he purposed to take his bride on a pilgrimage to this enchanted lake, which lay far to the northeast. He planned the trip with special attention to timing, for neither he nor his bride could miss Lucky Star's wedding.

The rules of proper courtship were strictly obeyed, and Two Shadows kept his visits with Black Feather short and well chaperoned, but they did manage to spend some time alone with each other. They had much planning to do, and Two Shadows commenced to build them a lodge and devise a plan as to how to provision their new dwelling with the proper furnishings of a home. They were as all young couples and limited on their budget. Two Shadows only had so much to trade for these essentials, but there was the trapping season. Gifted Hand had schooled him well, and the young man worked a hundred-mile trap line to the limits of human endurance. By the end of the season, he had enough furs to trade with the French and English to make his honeymoon lodge fit for Black Feather. There would be no luxuries, but the essentials were covered.

The living gift from Lucky Star, the yellow wolf-dog, had turned out to be a noble companion for Two Shadows. Star was a natural hunter, being part wolf, and the dog helped him in every aspect of hunting and trapping. The dog retrieved every downed bird and had a nose that could track any animal. He was not only intelligent but also completely in step with the will of Two Shadows. Star could anticipate what he should do next. Two Shadows and the wolf-dog came to know each other's thoughts without one word or sound or gesture between them, but Two Shadows did teach him how to follow hand signals and also how to sneak and crawl low to the ground, so as to sneak up and surprise game. It was a marvel to watch them working together. Star was gentle around other dogs and children, but when he sensed danger, he could be fearsome. The dog was large and heavily muscled and could also carry or pull a heavy load. Two Shadows employed his strength many times to help haul bundles of furs and loads of traps and bait. Star was a silent partner and had been taught to bark only once to warn Two Shadows of any impending danger.

Spring finally arrived. Their wedding day heralded an impressive gathering of the tribes and the Chippewa, Lakota Sioux, and the Cheyenne were well accounted. The ceremony included three days of feasting, games and goodwill, and to date, no one could remember a finer wedding celebration. The event brought the war chiefs of all three tribes together, and they truly embraced each other's company. Everyone gathered to give the bride and groom a heartfelt send-off, and the young couple departed upon the most worthy of gifts—Gifted Hand's best war ponies and with Buffalo Thunder's strongest pack horse. Star traveled in front, making certain the path to Gitche Gumee.

It was an epic journey, taking all of twelve days, but there was no trouble along the way. The entire route had been well planned by Two Shadows and Gifted Hand, and the bridal couple only traveled on age-old Chippewa trails and well within territory controlled by the tribe. Finally, one sunny, cloudless day, they climbed an impressive ridge that guarded the approach to the lake of legend. When they reached the summit, they looked out upon a blue sky expanse that went on and on, seemingly forever. They dismounted and found a rocky, treeless vantage point. They sat side-by-side, with Star nestled between them. Black Feather said, "It's so incredible that it brings tears to my eyes."

"Yes, the Great Spirit is in this place, just as he was the night of the shooting stars." Two Shadows embraced both his bride and Star, and they remained in reverent silence, letting time move on without a whisper.

The afternoon sun prompted Two Shadows, and he finally ended their reverie. "Let's move on down the mountain and set up camp next to that river, the one that flows into the lake. Tomorrow morning, I'll catch us some trout for breakfast."

Camp set up, fire set, Two Shadows observed as Black Feather arranged the buffalo robes for their bed. She removed her buckskins and moccasins and stretched out upon the robes. He looked upon her as one would study a sculpture or a beautiful sunset, yet no work of art had ever had this impact upon any man. All his previous life melted away to this moment; no shooting stars or perfect place upon this earth could compare to this present instant. There are times when a single heartbeat held an eternity. Black Feather turned and saw him. She smiled, extended her hand, and Two Shadows fell into her embrace. Men had fallen before into the great waters of Gitche Gumee, surrendering their lives; others had disappeared in blinding snows; more had been swept away by the whirlwinds of summer; yet none had so completely lost themselves as Two Shadows to Black Feather.

They spent the next ten days in paradise, loving each other, and daily giving thanks and honor to the Great Spirit. Their blessed time had drawn to a close, but their memories of Gitche Gumee would last every day for the rest of their lives. Now it was time to return home. Their honeymoon lodge awaited, and so did the wedding of their best friend, Lucky Star.

The yellow wolf-dog announced their return to the Seven Sisters village, and everyone turned out to greet the newest family in the tribe. The Chippewa had been busy during the young couple's absence. Everyone in the tribe contributed at least one article to the honeymoon lodge. The gifts included blankets, buckskins and buffalo robes, cooking utensils, stacked and split firewood, large earthenware jars filled with wild rice and corn flour, and baskets of dried fish, potatoes, and smoked venison. The old war chiefs had also spoken. Gifted Hand fashioned a baby cradle, then he filled a reed basket, woven by Moon Song, with new arrows. They were tipped with his finest and sharpest obsidian points. Buffalo Thunder honored Two Shadows by personally delivering a new musket, flints, black powder, and lead shot.

The young braves surrounded the returning newly weds and led their horses to the honeymoon lodge. The couple dismounted and, with everyone's urging, went in to investigate the tepee. They came out smiling and waving at the crowd, grateful beyond the telling. The braves unloaded and tended to the horses then settled them for the night. Two Shadows and Black Feather retired for the evening—filled with joy at being a part of The People. Star curled up on his own buffalo robe, taking up his position between the young couple and the universe beyond.

Soon enough, the day came to depart for Lucky Star's wedding. Most of the tribe made the journey. What a congregation it would be: the Lakota Sioux, most of their Cheyenne allies, and the Seven Sisters Chippewa band! Such a gathering had not been seen since the great peace powwow brought about by Buffalo Thunder and Gifted Hand. The bride groom, Dusty Swan, was a good man with an affable spirit, and he was deeply in love with Lucky Star. He was known to Two Shadows; in fact, he had ridden right next to him the day that they charged the Pawnee warriors. Dusty Swan had taken an arrow to his right foot and still walked with a limp. That made him and Two Shadows blood brothers, having both been wounded in the same campaign.

The wedding feast and celebration lasted four days, and in the end, the four young people were the last to say good-bye. Lucky Star hugged Black Feather; Dusty Swan embraced Two Shadows. Little did they know how much this friendship would come to serve them. Lucky Star kneeled down in front of the wolf-dog, saying, "May the Creator of all there is strengthen you to protect the ones I love."

New trails awaited, and the season of love had seen its first harvest.

13

Shades of Autumn

Words do not exist to capture how good life was for Black Feather and Two Shadows. The summer had been nearly perfect, the harvest bountiful. Their stores of earthenware jars and bowls were filled to the overflowing; the fishing had been the best in years, and the early season duck hunting proved great sport for Two Shadows and his partner, the wolf-dog, Star.

Black Feather was blessed, just as the seasons. She would bear their firstborn child in the spring. They felt showered; it seemed as though the Great Spirit had poured out his love upon them, and word had reached them that Dusty Swan and Lucky Star had invited them for a visit before snow season. They quickly made provision to take leave of their lodge and their people, and to join with their best friends at the Lakota Sioux village. Because Lucky Star was an Indian princess and daughter of the chief, her Cheyenne husband had chosen to make their home with the Sioux. His tribe had released him, and it was by way of honoring their alliance.

The large scale threat from the Pawnee was ameliorated, at least for the foreseeable future, but on the western Buffalo Prairie, there remained the danger of running into small raiding parties of Pawnee and their ally, the Shoshone. On the southern buffalo range, upon the wintering grounds, the Sioux also had to remain on guard against war parties of Comanche. In the center of their range and to the east, with the Chippewa, the Lakota were now at peace. To the north lay the dominion of the Cree, but the Sioux and Chippewa ventured into the far North Country only to trade at the French outpost. The Cree would not attack them while they were engaged in trade; it served Cree interests, but they were never welcome to linger in Cree territory.

Encroachment into the other Indian nation's territory only occurred by treaty or through warfare. The borders were not drawn on a map, and they overlapped, so some warring was always in the wind. The braves were compelled to go about the business of hunting and gathering, but at all times, they were prepared to engage in battle. That's the way it was with the tribes during the first autumn of the married life of Two Shadows and Black Feather.

The young couple, escorted by Star, entered the Lakota Sioux encampment and was immediately greeted by Dusty Swan and Lucky Star. The yellow dog ran to Lucky Star, stood upon his hind legs, his front paws on her shoulders, and washed her face most thoroughly.

"Get down, Star," ordered Two Shadows.

"I forgot how really big he is," said Lucky Star as she struggled face-to-face with the 120-pound wolf-dog to keep her balance. Star obeyed and returned to his master's side.

Dusty Swan announced, "Follow us and we'll see that you are settled in our lodge, and then I'll tend to your horses. Your dog can sleep in our tepee. He is welcome too."

Black Feather and Lucky Star embraced, and Lucky Star studied her face. "You are with child… I can see it in your eyes. I am so glad for you both!"

Black Feather was a little embarrassed, and her face flushed. She responded, "My time is in the spring."

The couples, reunited once again, enjoyed an evening of conversation, stories, and good food. Two Shadows talked a lot about duck hunting, and Dusty Swan shared some memorable buffalo hunts. They reveled in each other's hunting stories. Their ladies tired of the man talk and adjourned by themselves to speak of gentler topics. They sat side by side well into the night, speaking quietly and laughing frequently. They began to engage in traditional and simple pleasures. They busied their hands as they were talking, with beadwork on buckskin garments for the new baby. The men paused from their boastful tales to view their wives. They both had a sense of how truly blessed they had been to start out their life with such extraordinary brides. The evening was the most pleasant of reunions.

The next morning, the men would join a large hunting party; they were going after the king of the prairie, the buffalo. The women would remain behind, and they prayed over their husbands and blessed them and then sent them off well provisioned for their weeklong adventure.

As the hunting party traveled west and disappeared from view, Black Feather asked, "Don't you worry when they go after buffalo?"

"The Great Spirit has our husbands, and you and me, in the palm of his hands. In all things and no matter what happens, he will always be there for us. Just look at what he has done for you and for me already."

Black Feather gazed upon the countenance of Lucky Star and said, "Yes. He has allowed us to become sisters. You are such a wise and noble friend. I hope nothing will ever change between us."

"The seasons will have their way, but I, too, hope some things will never change."

By the end of the week, the men had returned with the bounty of a successful hunt. Their pack ponies each trailed a travois loaded to the limit with buffalo meat and skins. The men, too, were bursting to tell the tales of the hunt.

The young foursome enjoyed each other's companionship for two more days until the first snow began to fall. It was time to say good-bye, and they all agreed to meet again in the spring to celebrate the new baby. Now the seasons dictated their time. They had much buffalo meat to render and make ready for the smoking racks, and there were many buffalo skins to stretch and scrape and transform into usable robes. But working side by side, each couple was more than able to face the winter, and they all looked forward to the miracles of spring and to that time when they could be together once again.

14

Revelation

Two Shadows added twenty miles to his trap line that winter, motivated by the added responsibility of his coming child. He had entrusted his grandparents, Moon Song and Gifted Hand, to look in on his expectant wife. They were honored and did so faithfully and joyfully.

The trapping season was again bountiful, and the young father-to-be had bales of beaver skins and muskrat and mink pelts to take to the French traders. He said many prayers of thanks to the Great Spirit and also petitioned the Creator of all there is to allow him time to sell his furs and return home before the baby came.

The seasons turned once more; most of the snow had melted, and the ice was breaking up on the lakes. It was time for Two Shadows to load his pack horses with furs and journey north.

He carried his musket across his lap as he led his string of ponies. The rifle had more killing power than an arrow and could stop a charging bull moose or an enemy brave dead in their tracks. The weapon was .50 caliber and fired a lead ball as big as your thumb. Two Shadows rarely fired the gun. He was more inclined to hunt with his traditional weapons: his bow and arrows and his war lance spear. He could fire eight arrows on target in the same amount of time as he could fire and reload the musket once. If enemy braves attacked, he would fire his gun first and then switch to the bow and arrows and, lastly, his war club. Two Shadows was a thinking man, a cautious man. It was essential for him to return to his new family, as he now had responsibilities greater than himself. He had thought through his response to an attack.

The journey took six days on horseback, traveling from daylight until dark. Finally, Two Shadows could see the smoke coming from campfires inside the walled stockade of the fort. He waved at the French sentry above the gate and was promptly given access to the stockade.

The language barrier was no problem for the different Indian nations or for the French traders. There was one universal tongue between them all: hand signals. It was simpler than speech but could carry the message without any confusion. Sign language was the language of the times. The English were the only ones who would not use sign language. They were too proud and either relied on interpreters, or they expected the tribes to learn English.

Two Shadows enjoyed parlaying with the French. They welcomed him and treated him fairly as one would treat a brother. Two Shadows had come to like the French and trust them just as his grandfather, Gifted Hand.

The negotiations were swift and fair. The French agent, Andre Bouvier, asked Two Shadows for a favor: Would he take two foreigners to his tribe for a visit? He motioned to the back room of the fur trading warehouse, and two white people stepped forward, a young man and woman. The man addressed Two Shadows in English, extended his hand to greet him, and said, "I am Shawn Scott, and this is my wife, Rylee Morgan Scott. I am an artist and a writer, and my ambition is to record in my drawings the Indian way of life so that the people across the great waters will come to know about you and your people."

Andre Bouvier made sign language to relay the message, and Two Shadows shook the man's hand.

"I will pay you the sum of two one-hundred pound bales of beaver skins if you will allow me one week with your tribe," Scott proposed.

Two Shadows thought for a while and asked Bouvier, "How will he speak to us without signs?"

The Frenchman responded, "He can draw a picture on paper that is as clear as any sign, and he and his wife are both learning to sign. Very soon, they will succeed."

Two Shadows said, "Show me his drawings."

The French trader did so, presenting the brave with one of Scott's sketchbooks. Two Shadows studied the drawings. "I can promise only one week with my tribe, then I will escort you both back to the French post."

"Then the bargain is made," said Andre Bouvier, laughing, and they all celebrated with freshly made doughnuts and coffee—a rare delicacy to Two Shadows.

Upon their return to the Seven Sisters Chippewa village, the strangers were met with mixed reactions: curiosity and fear. There had never been a white person in their camp, and there was a certain dread of the unknown. All in the tribe had heard stories of white men, and many of the stories were not favorable. If it were not for Two Shadows's high standing in the tribe, the white couple might not have survived their incursion into Chippewa territory. Gifted Hand had dealt with both the French and English many times, so he welcomed the chance to get to know these two young foreigners. He had always harbored an inquisitive mind, and there might be much to learn from the visitors; at the very least, they could tell him of their people and what they thought and how they lived across the great waters.

Moon Song and Black Feather took the young lady under their wings, and Rylee Morgan Scott was to live in the lodge of Two Shadows and Black Feather. Her husband, Shawn, would bunk with Gifted Hand and Moon Song. Gifted Hand would see to it that Shawn Scott would have his opportunity to record on paper the ways of the Chippewa, and that if the Scotts wished it, their visit could be extended well beyond the promised week.

Rylee Morgan was a quick study, and by the end of the month, she had mastered sign language and also many common phrases in the Chippewa tongue. Her husband had diligently documented the everyday life of the people and had filled three sketchbooks with inspired and marvelously rendered drawings and watercolor paintings. Some day, all of England, Ireland, Scotland, and France would hold the drawings and stories in their hands. The newspapers would publish every scrap of information about the New World's native peoples.

The long-awaited day came for Black Feather and Two Shadows, and to them, a son was born! The entire tribe was overjoyed, no one more so than Rylee Morgan Scott—she had come to love Black Feather and her grandmother, Moon Song. Scott was born the same year and the same month as Black Feather; they were sisters in time.

Two Shadows and Gifted Hand were almost speechless with joy. To them, the seasons had come round with the gift of promise—what a life this child would lead. The boy would be taught by great men, thinking men. He would learn all things known to the tribe, how to live and love and fight, if necessary, and to honor the Creator of all there is.

A new thing also came with the visitors from afar: Rylee Morgan Scott and Shawn Scott told them about another birth long ago and far away. They shared the story of the baby Jesus, of his life and times, and of his importance to all The People. This was an eventful turning for the Chippewa tribe, one that would serve as a new beginning as well as an ending of many things. It was fated to be a bittersweet revelation.

Gifted Hand had set aside one afternoon to speak to Shawn Scott. Rylee Morgan Scott, by virtue of her gift for sign language and the Chippewa tongue, would assist in the conversation. Two Shadows, Black Feather, Moon Song, and the new baby also were present during this most important exchange. Gifted Hand lay the matter before him, "How do your people live across the waters, and why are they coming to our lands?"

Shawn Scott paused just long enough to carefully consider his response and then said, "Most of our people live in small villages or on isolated farms. In the countryside, we live with the land and raise cattle and sheep, chickens, and ducks. Some of our most important crops are gifts from your Indian peoples—the tribes of the east, the Iroquois, and the Delaware. They gave to us corn, squash, carrots, and, most importantly, potatoes.

"The village people do many crafts, and the clothing that we wear is made from the wool of sheep. Our boots and shoes are made from the rawhide leather of cattle. The musket that Two Shadows carries was made by our skilled gunsmiths. So you see most of our people are simple farmers or skilled artisans. Our ambition, then and now, is to live a humble and godly life and to enjoy the pleasure of family and friends in peace.

"We come to your land to escape injustice and worship our Creator as we see fit. Powerful and evil men rule in our lands, and they steal our crops and our cattle and try to force us to believe as they do. There is much bloodshed and conflict in our lands. We will not long endure these outrages against our people. That is why we come to the New World, to your world."

Rylee Morgan Scott made her husband's words quite clear to Gifted Hand. He was still filled with questions but wise enough to say no more.

The time had come for Two Shadows to fulfill his bargain and return the Scotts to the French trading post. The couple left with regret but also with an open invitation to return again someday. They had forged a permanent friendship with Gifted Hand, Moon Song, Black Feather, and Two Shadows.

15

Naming

The People understood the power of words and took special care in giving their child a name. Most babies and toddlers were given a childhood name that matched some characteristic of their personality. Later on, as they grew into young adulthood, some might merit a different name that could only be earned by some noteworthy act or noble deed.

Two Shadows wished to send word to Lucky Star and Dusty Swan to come for an important visit: to have an honored part in naming their newborn child. But first, out of respect, his grandfather was consulted. Gifted Hand agreed and asked Two Shadows to invite Buffalo Thunder as well. The old war chiefs could continue on with their conversations about the future of their two tribes. So the seeds of reunion were planted—all anticipating a golden harvest.

The day came, and their invited guests arrived at the Seven Sisters encampment. This time, it was Black Feather who rightly discerned that her best friend was with child! Lucky Star exclaimed, "Midwinter." The women were so excited that they began to chatter like a pair of song birds. Dusty Swan and Two Shadows quickly excused themselves and escorted their most honored guest, Buffalo Thunder, to the lodge of Gifted Hand. The old men looked upon each other with respect, and then Buffalo Thunder joined Gifted Hand in his lodge. They sat down upon buffalo robes, and after a splendid lunch prepared by Moon Song, they passed the peace pipe back and forth unhurriedly. Then they shared an afternoon of storytelling.

The young people tactfully adjourned so that they could all see the new baby. He was two months old now and very alert. He followed everyone's movements attentively and smiled and giggled when Lucky Star picked him up for the first time. The boy already focused his attention upon Star, the wolf-dog, and Star hovered near the child. It was even difficult for Two Shadows to entice the dog into his favorite pastime: riding along in the canoe for a day of fishing. Star seemed most content now while watching over the baby. Even Two Shadows had to restrain himself in rough housing with his boy. If Star perceived the game had gone too far, he would firmly grasp Two Shadows by the wrist with his impressive set of canines and growl. It was time to stop the mock wrestling and all fooling aside. The dog's antics made both the baby and his father break out into laughter. Two Shadows played along and set the baby back down in his crib, and then he growled back at Star and gave him a big bear hug. This routine always made the baby squeal with delight.

After a day and a half of just enjoying each other's company, Black Feather asked Lucky Star, "What do you think of names?"

Lucky Star did not immediately answer. She had been observing the baby, who was now singing and cooing in his own little universe. She inquired, "Does the baby sing like that often?"

Both Black Feather and Two Shadows answered at the same time and with the same word, "Always!"

"He seems to be a most happy spirit—he sings like a little cricket," observed Lucky Star.

Two Shadows smiled and removed the baby from the crib, hefting him up high above his head, saying, "Cricket—that's what we'll call you. Maybe someday you'll earn a mighty name of valor, but for now, you are our Cricket. What do you think, Black Feather?"

"Yes, I've always loved the songs of crickets. Do you remember the night of the shooting stars? The crickets pointed the way."

"I have not forgotten," said Two Shadows, and he passed Cricket to Lucky Star.

Gifted Hand asked the whole group to his lodge on the third day of their visit for a midday meal and an afternoon of conversation. This was an honor to the young people and could prove to be a most important exchange of ideas. They welcomed the invite.

After the meal and some simple conversation about the baby's new name, Gifted Hand offered up a topic for which he had invested much personal meditation. "What did you think of our recent guests, the Scotts?" (Gifted Hand had previously described in detail to Buffalo Thunder the events of the foreigner's stay with the Chippewa.)

"They had a good heart, and both walked the path of a true human being," said Two Shadows. Obviously, he had also given the matter much thought.

Black Feather offered, "I am curious about what they said regarding the Great Spirit. They said he had a son who came to live with the people in the form of a man, both man and God at once."

"Yes, and they also said all men are bad and that they could never see or be with the Great Spirit after their death unless they made peace with the son of God who they called the Jesus."

Dusty Swan thought on these things, as they were all new to him, and he said, "Are all men bad? I can agree that some of our enemies are very bad and without honor or mercy, but do not most men strive to walk in the way of the people? If they walk in the path of a true human being, will they not go to live with our fathers and with the Great Spirit? This new idea of the son of God is very troubling for me."

Buffalo Thunder finally spoke, "From the time that I was a young brave, my father took me along to trade furs with the French. There was always a priest present at the trading post, and we have heard this same message many decades ago. If the foreigners all follow this son of God, who is supposed to bring peace and justice into the world, why are the white people so troublesome to our people? They never seem satisfied—they always want more. It seems that they have no love for our land or for the way of the people. Do they not follow their own teachings, or are their teachings false? I don't know the answer. But here is my thought: if the young couple named Scott still remains at the French trading post, I would see them come to our Lakota village. Let us reason together and come to understanding."

"You have spoken wisely. None here know the answer. How would you invite the foreigners?"

Buffalo Thunder turned to Two Shadows and asked, "Would you go to the French post and escort the foreigners to our camp?"

Without hesitation, the brave promised, "I will, great Chief!"

The guests departed; it had proved a visit to remember, with great tidings in the wind.

16

Death on the Trail
Life in the Word

There was little time to waste in fetching the Scotts for Buffalo Thunder. It was midsummer, and Two Shadows would have to sacrifice much to make the journey. It was six days to the French fort and then seven days to the Lakota village and one day more home. He had much to do at home, with his young wife and child depending upon him to provision them for the coming winter. He was glad that he had the wolf-dog. Star would take the edge off the journey. The dog was his best friend and companion now, and they rarely were out of sight of each other, except when Star was watching over his wife and son.

Two Shadows had no furs to trade, so the French sentry was reluctant to let him and his wolf-dog pass. Finally, Andre Bouvier was summoned, and he recognized Two Shadows. Luck, so far, was with the brave. The Scotts had just returned the day before from a month-long visit with the Iron Lake Cree tribe where Shawn Scott had been engaged in his quest to document the tribes.

"Hello, Two Shadows," said Rylee Morgan Scott with flawless Chippewa. The brave and Shawn Scott shook hands. Andre Bouvier invited them all inside the fur buying warehouse for a parlay. Two Shadows was anxious to get back on the trail again, so he laid the matter before them, "Buffalo Thunder, war chief of the Lakota Sioux, has commissioned me to invite you for an extended visit. He instructs me to say that you can freely go about your business of drawing pictures of his people in exchange for more information about the one you call the true son—the Jesus."

The Scotts turned to each other and spoke for a moment in their own tongue, then Rylee Morgan turned to Two Shadows, saying, "We can be packed and ready to leave in one hour."

Andre Bouvier and Two Shadows enjoyed coffee and doughnuts once again to pass the time. Bouvier was sorting out and grading furs, and he handed a large wolf pelt to the brave. Two Shadows blew upon the long fur, and it rippled with supple elegance. He showed the hide to Star, but the wolf-dog looked away. Two Shadows handed the prime fur back to Bouvier and said, "The death of our brother gives us no pleasure."

"We are ready!" Rylee Morgan announced. Two Shadows checked their horses and gear and noticed that Shawn Scott also carried a musket slung from a scabbard within easy reach on the right side of his horse. He asked, "Is it loaded?"

"It is, and I am a very good shot. Are you expecting trouble?"

Rylee Morgan served as an interpreter between the men. "I never expect anything, but it is a good thing to be wary whenever you are away from home." And with that comment, Two Shadows and Star led the group on their first steps toward destiny.

Toward the evening of the first day, as Two Shadows was scouting for a place to make an overnight camp, Star began to growl. Two Shadows held out a hand signal, and Star went silent. Two Shadows dismounted and motioned to the Scotts to stay where they were, and he and Star began to circle and crawl through heavy brush to investigate. Two warriors were well hidden next to the trail ahead and poised with their muskets to ambush the Scotts. Two Shadows tapped Star and bared his teeth. The dog understood and barked once. One of the warriors spun round with his musket and fired. He shot a hole right through one of Star's ears. The dog charged the assassins but not before Two Shadows had fired his musket, nearly cutting the shooter in half.

The second warrior dashed to his horse, gave out a fearful war whoop, and was gone before Star could pull him down. Shawn Scott called out, and Two Shadows said one of his few English words, "Aye!"

They all quickly assembled over the body of the fallen warrior. Shawn Scott looked upon the dead man and said, "I know this man, Noir Metis! He is one of two brothers, both bad medicine. They are mixed bloods—half Cree and half French and loyal to neither. They are criminals and renegades and have reigned terror, robbing and murdering in Cree, Sioux, and Chippewa territory. They have killed French and English, and they carry a large bounty on their head. We would have to take his body back to the fort for you to claim the reward, but remember this, the brother, Bonne Metis, will be out to kill you now. It's too bad he escaped."

"I won't take any reward for killing a man. We'll bury him where he lays. You can keep his horse and weapons for a gift to the Lakota," said Two Shadows, and then the brave tended to the wound in Star's ear. It wasn't serious and would heal, but it left a hole the size of a man's thumb through his right ear.

The remainder of the journey was uneventful, but as he rode upon his horse, swaying gently with the animal's movements, he considered a new reality. He now had a blood enemy, a skilled man of war sworn to vengeance. Bonne Metis would now pose a constant menace no matter where Two Shadows traveled. He had indeed sacrificed much to bring the Scotts to Buffalo Thunder.

They finally arrived, and after introductions and greetings all around, Two Shadows acquainted Buffalo Thunder with the account of their journey. The war chief listened attentively and examined the wound in Star's ear and then said, "I know of Bonne Metis and his brother, Noir Metis, the one you killed. These are very bad men. They have also murdered Sioux braves just to steal furs and horses. Too bad you did not kill them both. But enough talk of death. Let me show all of you to my lodge, and we can eat and you can rest. My people will tend to the horses. Come now."

Two Shadows said, "I can only remain until midday tomorrow. I must return to my wife and child."

Fully fed and rested, the group woke up to a bright late summer day filled with new promise. As they shared a meal, Buffalo Thunder spoke to the Scotts. He asked them, "How is it that you say all men are bad and that no one is worthy to join the Great Spirit except by a peace treaty with the Jesus? This seems a hard thing to my people. We have many good men who walk rightly in the way of the people. We do not understand this new thing."

"You have spoken well, Buffalo Thunder," said Shawn Scott, and his wife, Rylee Morgan, began to translate by sign language. Scott continued, "In the times of Jesus, just as now across the great waters, many bad kings ruled the land, and all the people were compelled to follow and obey the kings. Among your people, you would call them war chiefs. There were a few good kings who were recognized by the Great Spirit as men who walked the true path of the people. But even the good kings did some wrong things, which separated them from the will of the Great Spirit. So the Great Spirit, the Creator of all there is, made a way for all men to never be separated from him again. He sent his one true Son, Jesus, to be a ruler and king over the people. Jesus never did any wrong thing, so by following him in life, the people could be led all the way to heaven…and upon their death, they could spend all time at the home of the Great Spirit. Only through the son can we come to Father. In the end, Jesus exchanged his life for our bad deeds."

Buffalo Thunder thought good and long upon these words and finally said, "It is a hard thing you say—we must talk much over the coming days, as I do not yet understand."

"We have time," said Shawn Scott.

"My time has come full circle," said Two Shadows, and after good-byes all around, he took his leave and began the day long journey home.

17

Dreamtime

Moon Song was the first to see Two Shadows. She greeted Star and started to pet his head with both hands. The wolf-dog whined when she touched his right ear. "What has happened to Star?"

"Trouble on the trail," answered Two Shadows, but he did not elaborate.

By then, more of the tribe had gathered, and Black Feather appeared, carrying Cricket, and she ran to her husband. It was so good to be home at last. He held his wife and baby tightly, and she knew that something was wrong. Everyone had questions for him, but Two Shadows needed rest. He said, "I will meet tomorrow morning with Gifted Hand and with any of you who are interested and share my journey." Then he tended to his horse, entered his lodge, and settled in for the evening. He stretched out on the buffalo robes, still dressed in his buckskins, and without eating, he was soon fast asleep. The dog rested his head on Two Shadows's stomach, his prodigious form also covering half of his chest. No one, not even Black Feather or the baby, would be allowed tonight.

Two Shadows began to dream—and this was more than a dream. He saw a man clothed in white and as bright as the sun. He was too radiant to look upon. He held out his hand and said, "Follow." Then the image of the man in white was gone. There came another vision, the face of death. This image did not speak; it just stared at Black Feather and Cricket and Two Shadows. It was the face of Bonne Metis! Then the dream visions ceased, and Two Shadows fell into a deep slumber.

Two Shadows did not awaken until midmorning. Star was still there, covering him. The baby was singing and lying right next to Star, playing and tugging at his paws. Black Feather was seated next to them, busily working upon the decorative beadwork fringe on a new pair of heavy knee-high winter moccasins, a special gift to honor her true love. The moccasins were double walled, compartmented, and filled with wool, a rare gift from the Scotts. They would serve to keep him warm and dry, as the outside was thoroughly sealed with mink oil for the long trapping season ahead. What a scene to wake up to! Suddenly, he stood up with a start, and the dog also jumped to his feet. Two Shadows had remembered the visions, but he said nothing; instead, he placed his hands on Black Feather's cheeks, bent down, and gave her an embrace. Then he picked up his son and said, "What's for breakfast?"

The meal served; he undressed, washed himself all over, then put on his best buckskins. He was going to meet his grandfather and the tribe, and he would do so with respect.

The people were eagerly awaiting his presence; they all loved to hear a new story. Stories were the stuff that life was made from. They were magical and the tie that binds among The People. They were the currency of time and a payment of sorts for a life richly lived.

Two Shadows greeted Gifted Hand and Moon Song. His grandmother brought out the buffalo robes and spread them in front of their tepee. This was a public gathering as all in the tribe had a stake in what Two Shadows would say. The men were seated, and their family and the rest of the tribe gathered around and also sat down. "Tell us of your passage," said Gifted Hand.

Two Shadows gave the people a detailed account of his fourteen-day odyssey, leaving nothing out. He even told them of the visions of last night, which he also considered as a part of the same journey. When he finished, he called to Star, and the dog quickly appeared by his side. "See his wound? The dog may well have saved all our lives." Two Shadows gently lifted the wolf-dog's ear so that all could see, and the crowd *oohed* and *aahed*.

Gifted Hand sat quietly, thinking over each of Two Shadows's words. The matter of Bonne Metis was troubling, and the old man was totally aware of the danger that the evil man presented to his grandson and also to his great-grandson. No one in Two Shadows's family would be truly safe until Bonne Metis was dead. The other matter—the word about the Jesus—was also troubling. Gifted Hand and his people, through all the ages, had a very personal walk with the Great Spirit. All things held a spirit, man, animals, birds, trees, even the wind. Who could rightly say that a bear or a wolf or a raven had no spirit? Who could say that the Creator of all there is did not hold the seasons and his people in the palm of his hand? This new thing, this one way only through the son of God, was most troubling. Did the white man truly follow this Jesus? They seemed to never be at peace—they always lusted for more. More land, more furs, and more power. Maybe the Scotts were the key. They had earned the trust of both the Lakota and the Chippewa, and they had asked for but one thing: to tell the story of The People to the foreigners across the great waters. Gifted Hand finally spoke, "The man called Shawn Scott and his wife, Rylee Morgan, left me with a present. It is a book of words by the Great Spirit. One of our tribe should learn to read these words so that we will come to know the truth, from the voice of the Creator of all there is himself. We can trust no man to talk this talk. Who among you will learn these words?"

"I will, Grandfather, but who will teach me?" Black Feather proclaimed.

No one had an answer, and the meeting was concluded. The people all went on about their business, preparing for the season of snows once again.

18

Something New from Something Old

Winter came with an unholy fury that year—sub-zero temperatures for weeks at a time and more snow than Two Shadows had ever seen. He was forced to cut his trap line to a paltry 30-mile circle instead of last year's 120 mile line. Even Star found it hard going, and the weather was just too severe to use the ponies. There wasn't enough food on the snow-covered trail for them to survive. Two Shadows, by virtue of his snowshoes, could manage, but Star regularly broke through the crust and bellied out in the deep snow. It became a backbreaking work for them, but the trapping was fair. There was one more thing: both Two Shadows and the wolf-dog knew they were being hunted. Star frequently stopped to scent the wind. They did not see anything, but both of them could feel the eyes of their enemy upon them. It was pure relief now every time they returned safely home to Black Feather and the baby.

It came time again for snowmelt, and Cricket had already started to walk and talk. Now he carried his happy songs all over the village, and everyone looked forward to his presence. Black Feather was as beautiful as ever, and she was the best mother and wife that Two Shadows had ever seen. She was also his best friend, along with Star, and the young couple spent part of each day just talking with each other. They took many walks around the village, hand in hand with each other and their son.

One lovely spring day, Gifted Hand came to their lodge for a visit. "Good morning to you all! I've brought you a jug of Moon Song's best maple syrup and a wood carving of Star for Cricket. I could not think of a worthier figure to make for the boy. I've also given the matter of the book of the words by the Great Spirit much thought. There is a lodge for visitors at the French trading post, and I'm sure that Andre Bouvier would allow you and your family to stay there at my request. I'm thinking that maybe Rylee Morgan could teach Black Feather how to read the English words."

"Do you know what you ask? I have been hunted by my enemy all winter. Do you expect me to expose my wife and child on the long trail to the French fort?"

"I have not forgotten. A dozen of our best warriors will escort you to the fort and upon your return."

Two Shadows said, "The French sentry will not let a war party pass."

Gifted Hand responded, "There is no need. Once at the fort, their mission is complete."

"What about the Cree? They might mistake our group as a raiding war party."

"I will send along the white peace belt, and if you run into the Cree, show it plainly, and they will let you pass, and besides, no one goes to war with their wife and child and a load of furs."

"Give us some time to consider your words, and we will let you know."

Gifted Hand had faith in his grandson and returned to his lodge to wrap the book in buckskin to protect it for the journey north. After a short interlude, Two Shadows arrived at his lodge and said, "We have both decided to honor your request. We will be ready to leave as soon as you assemble the braves." Gifted Hand did so, and the party left the next morning.

The Scotts were living at the lodge in the fort, and they were overjoyed when Two Shadows and his family arrived for their visit. Andre Bouvier moved them into the room adjacent to the Scotts'. Two Shadows and his family had never stayed in a white man's house before, and they were amazed at the feather beds and the fireplace, the wash basin and padded chairs, the kerosene lanterns and rugs on the floor. There was even a glass window to look out upon the courtyard of the busy fort. There was one more convenience, one that Two Shadows appreciated: a lock on the door.

Once his family was safely settled, Two Shadows stabled the horses and collected his furs and paid a visit to his friend, Andre Bouvier.

"Mon Amie, you are most welcome. Let us finish our trading…and then coffee and doughnuts."

A smile came to Two Shadows, and he shook hands with his friend. They quickly settled their account, sitting on either side of the trading counter, and talked of many things. Bouvier had heard about the bad business with the Métis brothers, and he told Two Shadows of the latest news. Bonne Métis had been robbing and raiding as far east as Gitche Gumee, but for the past month, his whereabouts was unknown. Bouvier asked his friend, "Why do you not claim the reward? The Scotts will attest that you dispatched Noir Métis."

"I want no blood money."

The matter was dropped, and the two men began to share many stories of trapping and hunting and of survival in the hard season just passed.

Rylee Morgan Scott and Black Feather spent most of their days and evenings together. By the end of the month, they had made an equal and worthy exchange: Black Feather could read English, and Rylee Morgan could speak a rudimentary Chippewa. Of course, there were many words that both of them did not know; this level of understanding might take several seasons of study and practice. With sign language, however, they were able to fill in the gaps of the difficult words and expressions.

Two Shadows was too antsy to stay indoors during the long sessions and left to walk around the fort or visit with Bouvier. The brave and Star even left the fort for short hunting excursions. Shawn Scott asked to accompany Two Shadows but was turned down. There was the ever present threat of attack. The brave almost wished it would happen, better now, with his family and friends safe inside the fort. But no suddenness occurred, and the Chippewa war party returned to escort them home again.

There was no trouble on the trail, and all were glad to be reunited at the Seven Sisters encampment. Life settled into a magical routine, gardening, fishing, working on craft projects, spending time with family. The little happy toddler was growing stronger every day and began to accompany his dad everywhere. He, along with Star, came to love fishing with Dad in the birch bark canoe. He liked to dip his hand in the water as they glided around on Spirit Lake. The little boy got so excited when they came upon loons or the Canada geese. He tried to talk to the birds, making his best imitation of their songs. Two Shadows observed with keen interest as his boy discovered his own, special spirit. Cricket loved the birds and animals, just as Black Feather.

The boy's mother asked Two Shadows for an unusual favor: she wanted some kind of food or grain to feed the wild birds. She also asked her husband to make a feeding station up off of the ground to care for her wild friends. He did so, scouring the fields and hills for seeds and berries. Then he made a two-level feeder, placing it just behind their lodge. Black Feather and Cricket came to spend part of each morning enjoying their birds, and Cricket learned to mimic many of their calls. He had a gift—a natural ear and voice. Many in the tribe marveled at this new thing.

With people as old as the Chippewa, who had lived with nature for untold centuries, Black Feather and Cricket had started a brand new tradition, and it caught on and spread to other families in their tribe.

By late summer, Gifted Hand attended these morning sessions, and Black Feather began to translate stories from the white man's book, the Bible. Gifted Hand would sit without speaking and listen to every word. Others in the tribe slowly joined with the group, and a new thing came to the tribe: morning story time. It was a sight to behold, Black Feather tending the birds, Cricket singing back and forth with them, and the Great Spirit feeding his flock.

Chapter 7: Myths, Monsters and Men

Chapter 10: Mountaintop

Chapter 11: The Gift

Chapter 13: Shades of Autumn

Chapter 16: Death on the Trail, Life in the Word

Chapter 18: Something New from Something Old

Chapter 24: Spirit Cave

Chapter 26: Signs and Wonders

Chapter 29: Saying Good-bye

Chapter 31: The Wicker Woman

Chapter 34: Sweet Air of Home

Chapter 35: The Whirlwind

19

Reckoning

Word had come that Lucky Star had given birth to a daughter. The news had reached the Chippewa camp early in the spring before Black Feather and her family had been obliged to leave for schooling at the French trading post. Black Feather wanted very much to visit her best friend and bring gifts, but Two Shadows was not willing to undertake the journey. It was just too risky. By the end of summer, nothing had changed, so the visit was indefinitely postponed.

The brave had tired of the dark cloud over them, tired of being a target. He resolved before the season of snow to settle with Bonne Métis. He would become the hunter. Bonne Métis had boasted all over the territory that he would take the scalp the man who had shot his brother to death. To prolong the evil, he was taking his sweet time. He felt a rush of power while observing Two Shadows from a distance. The renegade began to leave sign on the trail for his enemy to find—he was becoming expert at taunting his foe. In so doing, he had unconsciously revealed the warped workings of his mind to Two Shadows. Certain patterns began to emerge. Bonne Métis always observed from high ground and never moved down to the trails until well after dark to leave his calling cards. He always stayed downwind so that the wolf-dog could not home in on his hiding place. He traveled alone on one war pony. He never made a campfire nor hunted for food; he must have carried dried meat, jerky or pemmican. At night, he became invisible, sleeping in the tall grass and knocking down a small clearing just large enough for a blanket. Two Shadows had discovered more than one of these overnight hideouts after the fact. He would harass Two Shadows for three days and then leave for three weeks to employ his principal avocation: robbing and murdering across Chippewa lands.

Two Shadows had put together the signature of his enemy, and he had devised a plan. It gave him no pleasure to consciously become a hunter of men; it went against his own nature and the words that Black Feather had been teaching him from the book all summer. He liked the words from the book, but Two Shadows was a man with a family, a man who had to do things on occasion not of his choosing.

It was the prime season to hunt for deer, and he and Star headed for the large range of wooded ridges one day's ride to the northeast, a game-rich area. Two Shadows made a big show of setting up a base camp on the meadow below the tallest hill. It would coincide with the return of his enemy, as it had been three weeks since Métis had last dogged his trail. Two Shadows made a very large campfire and stockpiled a great cache of logs and wood, a scene sure to draw his enemy down from the summit. The brave did not make a night shelter, as was his custom; instead, he slept in the open on buffalo robes next to the blaze. He commanded Star to stay and covered up for the night.

Métis had been watching and was very amused that Two Shadows had been so reckless, letting his guard down in such a careless manner. In the middle of the night, with such a tempting and easy target, Bonne Métis made his move. He warily crept within close gun range, downwind of the wolf-dog and his sleeping master. He braced his musket across a fallen tree, took a deep breath, steadied his sights on Two Shadows's back, and fired. A cloud of dust rose when the bullet struck, and Two Shadows moaned. Métis didn't even bother to reload; he couldn't wait to start out after his war trophy—Two Shadows's scalp. He would finish off the wolf-dog with his knife and tomahawk and skin the dog as a bonus. Star did not charge Bonne Métis; he just stood his ground by Two Shadows's body, growling with hatred.

Métis yelled out, "Make all the noise you want, you stupid cur. I will kill you now and take your hide!"

At that instant, Two Shadows threw off his buffalo robe and sprang to his feet, taking aim at the stunned renegade's heart.

"But how?" Bonne Métis managed to say.

"Andre Bouvier made a vest of iron, front, and back, and he asked me to be sure to greet you!" Then Two Shadows pulled the trigger, and his enemy crumpled under a cloud of smoke. Two Shadows had to restrain Star, as the wolf-dog wanted to tear his enemy to pieces. The brave drug the carcass twenty paces to the fire, heaped more logs upon the blaze, and threw his body in the midst. This man deserved no prayers or ceremony, no marked place in the ground or upon a burial platform. His ashes would lie on unhallowed ground, a testimony to his evil life.

Two Shadows broke camp the next morning, and he and Star climbed to the top of the hill to his enemy's hideout and collected his war pony. He also collected all Métis's gear and weapons. He would keep the pony as fair exchange for the inconvenience that Métis had caused him, but he had other plans for the renegade's other possibles.

By late afternoon, Two Shadows had arrived home at the Seven Sisters encampment. He greeted his wife and child and then visited Gifted Hand at his lodge. He shared the last chapter in the story of Bonne Métis. He and Gifted Hand surveyed Métis's weapons and gear. They both agreed that it was fitting to send the weapons of war, as well as the iron vest, to Andre Bouvier for display above his trading counter. Perhaps Bouvier could make a sign warning all would-be renegades of their future. Then they spread the contents of Métis's saddle bags upon a buffalo robe. There were hundreds of gold coins—the fruits of a lifetime of plunder! Gifted Hand proposed, "How about a school at the fort for the children of all of the tribes—the Chippewa, the Sioux, and the Cree?"

"You have spoken wisely, Grandfather."

Gifted Hand ended the discussion with, "These trophies of war will be on their way within the hour. Two of our braves are leaving with furs for the French fort."

Now the time was right. Two Shadows invited his wife and son to join him for a journey to the Lakota Sioux stronghold. Their best friends and the new baby girl awaited. They would go bearing many gifts, including the new war pony of Métis, and they could travel in peace without the need to look over their back trail anymore. Star would lead the procession, taking his place of honor.

20
Harvest

Time was of the essence. It was the swing time of the year when winter could descend unexpectedly. The temperature could drop fifty degrees in one day, if winter arrived, or a traveler might leave on a sunny afternoon and wake up to a foot of snow. The autumn leaves were falling, and the visit to the Lakota village could have no more delay.

As the wolf-dog, Star, entered the Sioux stronghold, many people appeared to greet their delegation. Word had preceded them about Two Shadows's day of reckoning with their enemy, Bonne Métis, and the families who had lost sons to the renegade came bearing gifts for the victorious warrior. The French fur buyer, Andre Bouvier, had made an epic story of the battle. Every fur trade was accompanied by his animated tale as he pointed to the display of the outlaw's weapons and especially to the iron vest that had been his undoing. He also played up the role of the wolf-dog, making Star a legendary hero. Many of the Lakota Sioux braves had heard of the battle firsthand while marketing their furs.

Buffalo Thunder, Lucky Star, and Dusty Swan headed the welcome party. The guests were directly escorted to Dusty Swan's lodge. Two Shadows handed the reins of his former enemy's war pony to Dusty Swan, saying, "We honor the birth of your daughter with this trophy of war."

Dusty Swan took the reins and said, "Your safe return is gift enough, but we thank you for this honor." Lucky Star hugged Black Feather and Cricket and said, "Come and meet our daughter."

The seven-month old was crawling all about the floor of the tepee, getting stuck on the folds in the buffalo robes. She would struggle and fall over right herself and try again. She was very persistent. Black Feather observed, "She has a strong will and will not be discouraged."

Dusty Swan replied, "Please do us the honor of helping to arrive at a suitable name. We have awaited your visit for just this purpose."

Two Shadows said, "May the Creator of all there is open our eyes and show us your daughter's true spirit." Then the friends settled in for a meal and a long afternoon of rest and good stories. Cricket adored the baby girl and followed her around the lodge, smoothing out the buffalo robes and removing other obstacles from her path. He shared his wood carving of Star, but the baby was more interested in the wolf-dog himself. She tried to hug the dog, and he allowed it, but she came away with two fistfuls of his whiskers. The baby had a powerful grip, but Star ignored the pain and licked her face. The baby finally picked up the toy dog, and it made Cricket so happy that he began to sing. The baby squealed with joy, making the parents join in with laughter.

Buffalo Thunder arrived the next morning and inquired after Gifted Hand. Two Shadows responded, "When we left him, he was duck hunting by Spirit Lake, the happiest place on this earth."

Both the old war chiefs were entering that final season, and the times and their war wounds were leading them to the winter of their life. The brave added, "He asked me to greet you, and he sent the Scotts' book of words along so that Black Feather could share with you some of his select stories."

"I have heard of this book, and I look forward to hearing these words," said the old war chief.

Black Feather said, "Let us all sit together, and I will tell you one of Gifted Hand's favorites, of David and the giant." The group settled around her, even the babies, and she began, "Long ago there was a young brave tending his father's sheep. This child was destined some day to be a ruler over his people and a mighty war chief. A bear came to attack his lambs, and he struck him down with his sling. A sling is a leather strap that holds a stone and hurls the stone with lethal speed and accuracy, like the blow of a strong war club. A lion also came to kill the sheep, and David again struck him down. It came to pass that David's people were attacked by a large war party, and the king did not know what to do. The enemy was too large and strong for his warriors. The enemy was led by a powerful giant, who was a fearsome killer of men. This giant came every day and taunted David's king, challenging the king to send his best warrior to battle with him. No man dared, no man was worthy. One day, David came to the camp of his king to bring food to his brothers, who were soldiers in the king's service. He heard the taunts of the giant who insulted the king, his soldiers, and his God. The God of David's people was the Great Spirit, the one true Creator of all there is. David was filled with righteous anger and said to the king and to the giant, 'I will go!' No one believed in David, as he was but a young man, but no one else had enough courage. So the king sent him into battle. The giant mocked him and, once again, mocked his God and came forward to cut off David's head. David said, 'Who are you to defy the army of the living God?' The giant laughed him to scorn, but David pulled out a smooth, round stone and loaded his sling. He swung the sling round and round his head and loosed the stone. It flew straight and true, striking the giant in the midst of his forehead. The giant fell to the earth with a mighty crash! David went forward and, with the giant's own long knife, cut off his head. The army of David's king, the army of his God, had carried the day. The end."

"Did this battle truly take place?" Buffalo Thunder asked excitedly.

Black Feather replied, "Our friends, the Scotts have promised us that every word in this book is of the Great Spirit, they are true and are given to The People for all time."

Buffalo Thunder petted the wolf-dog, finally saying, "Over the coming days, I wish to hear more stories."

"Just as you wish, mighty Chief," said Black Feather.

The coming days were a special time. The young couples took walks around the village with their children and Star and just lived in the perfect autumn weather. It was sunny, warm, and calm—a perfect week for a visit. And once each day, Buffalo Thunder and his people came for story time, and the book once again beckoned.

The night before their friends were to leave, Lucky Star had a dream. She saw a woman clothed in white, with a purple covering over her head. The young lady glowed with a remarkable countenance, raised and extended her hand, palm forward, saying, "Your child shall point the way." Then she was gone. When Lucky Star awoke, she remembered the dream and told her guests. Lucky Star wondered aloud, "Who was she?"

Without hesitation, Black Feather replied, "Mary, the mother of Jesus."

"What do you think it means?"

"Your daughter has a calling, and the lady came to bless her. Your daughter will carry a message to her people."

"Messenger," said Dusty Swan, "that's a fine name! What do you think, Lucky Star?"

"Messenger, yes. It is a good name. We will call her Messenger."

And so it was, another season had come and gone, another journey fulfilled, a new chapter completed—and the fruits of friendship had delivered one more bountiful harvest.

21
Winds of Change

The fur trading post, the French fort, was becoming a hub of activity. The compound had expanded from the original fur trading outpost to include a mercantile store and a livestock yard, a church, a lodge with an inn, and, now thanks to Gifted Hand and Two Shadows, a language school for Indian children. A dormitory to house the children was also well under construction. The fort boasted permanent residents now and was taking on the appearance of a settlement. Hunters and trappers continued their trade as before, but new people were coming regularly to stay at the lodge while they undertook diverse activities in the area. Some came to the mercantile to purchase farm equipment and seed grain as well as sheep and cattle, ducks, and chickens. Some French and a small number of other nationalities were moving into the region to settle with their families. The Lakota Sioux and Chippewa observed these movements with some alarm. In the past, they had tolerated the few voyageur trappers and traders, but when men began to build houses, clear land, and bring their women, they did so upon Indian land, and the warriors were watching.

The Scotts had built a log home inside the fort as a base of operations for Shawn Scott's extended Indian studies. Rylee Morgan Scott, from the very outset, had faithfully documented native tongues. She had amassed stacks of research cards, with different keywords and phrases, as well as common signing hand gestures. She had begun assembling all of her notes into one book of translation. Rylee Morgan also assisted her husband in annotating each of his sketches and paintings. Once in Chippewa, Sioux, and Cree, his artwork would comprise a second, illustrated reference. This picture book could prove ideal for teaching the children, as they could recognize the scenes: gathering wild rice, tapping maple trees to make syrup, hunting buffalo, setting up tepees, spearing or netting fish, and so on. The children could readily associate the words with the activities portrayed.

Andre Bouvier and the Scotts managed one more significant coupe: they were able to convince both the French and English to release the bounty on the dead renegade, Métis brothers, to Two Shadows. The brave would keep no prize for besting these killers, so he immediately turned over this windfall of gold to the new children's school at the fort. The funds were sufficient to outfit the classroom and staff the school for a decade to come. It was left to Bouvier as the superintendent of the fur trading post to appoint the first administrator and teacher of the new school. He wisely filled the posts with Shawn Scott and his wife. Bouvier knew that the Scotts would be acceptable to the war chiefs.

So the school was built, the teachers in place, the translations complete, the business at hand…invite the children! Shawn Scott traveled to the Seven Sisters Chippewa stronghold to enlist Two Shadows into accompanying him on his mission. Scott had a good reason for selecting Two Shadows: he and his wolf-dog were well-known throughout the territory. The tribes had respect for this mighty warrior and his companion, Star. They had also heard that Two Shadows had given his bounty gold for the language school. The brave would be received as an honored guest, paving the way for Scott to recruit the children and gain the goodwill of their parents. The war chiefs of the tribes understood the wisdom of sending at least a few of their children. They needed to know what the foreigners were thinking. They either had to find ways to coexist, or there would be war. Such a war could escalate to an unprecedented scale.

When Scott made the proposal, Two Shadows replied, "Yes, you can rely on me."

Gifted Hand once again gave his grandson the peace belt to display across his arm. Shawn Scott replied, "I pray that this school becomes the seed for big things, good things, for all of The People."

Gifted Hand asked, "How many do you seek, and how long will they be at the fort?"

Scott replied, "Our goal is ten from each tribe, from the Chippewa, Lakota Sioux, and Cree. We will offer four years of winter classes, twelve weeks in length. At the end of four winters, the children will be able to read and converse in French and English. Some gifted students will be offered an additional four years of classes, and a select few may accompany my wife and me back to England and Scotland in eight years' time. My wife and I are planning a tour of our homeland and France to show our paintings and explain the life of The People. Our students will be invaluable as ambassadors of their tribes. The timing is right for the people across the great waters to know the truth about your way of life."

Gifted Hand thought upon these words and finally expressed his concern, "Will all of this contact between our peoples cause more foreigners to come?"

Shawn Scott had always been forthright with the war chiefs, and he replied, "Yes. More will come. But it is better for those who do come to have respect for The People and their ways. Good people can make good neighbors. Uninformed people, with no care or thought for the tribes, will lead to conflict. New people are going to come. Let us hope that understanding will make a true path."

Gifted Hand spoke no more, but the dread in the center of his being remained. He was wise and knew that change was in the wind. But no one truly knew what the future would bring.

He knew that no one among his people desired change. Then Shawn Scott, Two Shadows, and Star quietly departed on their epic journey.

22

Ties That Bind

Four years had passed, and the first class of students were about to graduate from *Nations Academy*. Not one of the thirty students had dropped out, and with varying degrees of success, each had learned to read and write in their own native language. About one-third of the students, who had a natural ear and an eagerness to learn, had also grasped the basics in both French and English. Their new facility for conversation was very rudimentary; proficiency would require time and practice. When the students finished their classroom studies each spring, Rylee Morgan Scott encouraged them to take home two books: the Bible and one book of their choice. In this way, their progress could continue.

The war chiefs of the Lakota Sioux, the Chippewa, and the Cree were well satisfied with the results. The Scotts had fulfilled their promise to the chiefs, made four years ago. Now the tribes could parlay with the foreigners, and everyone could openly discuss their intentions and concerns. The Chippewa and the Cree seemed open to a limited presence of the new immigrants in their territory. The Lakota Sioux, however, feared an invasion. Their holy men and war chiefs had seen visions of destruction by a sea of white men. Their way of life was the way of the buffalo, their survival linked together through the threads of time. They were obliged to travel unimpeded with the movements of the herds. Their nomadic way of life could easily be disrupted by those who would not revere the buffalo, by those who would obstruct the herds' seasonal migrations with fences, farms, and ranches. The

Sioux could not allow this to happen; they would fight to preserve their sacred tribal ways. The foreigners were also at odds with each other. The French and English were bringing their age-old feuds to the new world. Everyone could sense evil winds looming over the Indian nations.

Word had reached the war chiefs that some of the tribes of the east, by the great waters, were already in open conflict with the English. Never before had the chiefs a greater need to dialog with the French and English; to survive, they must know of their intentions. The new school, the Nations Academy, and the Scotts were smack in the middle of these intrigues.

The wolf-dog, Star, was in his prime, and Black Feather and Two Shadows's son, Cricket, was primed and eager for school at the French fort. It was late winter, nearly spring, and the family contingent was on the trail north to join their friends, the Scotts, for the graduation of the very first class. Dusty Swan, Lucky Star, and their seven-year-old daughter, Messenger, were also on their way. The old war chiefs, Buffalo Thunder and Gifted Hand, would soon join them. This was a first ever event, and it was big. They all had an interest in the success of the premiere graduating class. The war chief of the Cree would also be there.

Andre Bovier and the Scotts were at the gate to greet them in turn as they arrived. This was a meeting of best friends, and this time together would prove to be golden. Nine of the graduating students would return for four more winters. Music and arithmetic would be added to their continuing language studies. And twenty new children, Cricket and Messenger among them, would begin their four-year program of studies. Cricket and Messenger would have a leg up on the other children, as Black Feather had continued with story time for the children at every opportunity. Messenger had proved to have a sharp memory and could repeat the Bible stories flawlessly.

They were seated thusly: first the old war chiefs, then the children and their families, and lastly, the guests and the visitors from the fort. Superintendent Andre Bouvier introduced the Scotts, and they, in turn, one by one, called the children forth to receive their diploma. These certificates were like no other: they were made on buckskin, fringed with beads and tassels of horse hair depicting the image of a lake with a canoe bearing a single traveler. It signified their coming journey. The children received a hug from Rylee Morgan Scott and a blessing from Shawn Scott. The old chiefs watched and wondered. Many hopes traded before them, but the seasons would bear witness that some in this class would seek the path of the peace that passed all understanding, while others in this same class would be bruised by life, taking offense at their pain, and drift toward a path where there was no peace to be found.

When the ceremony was concluded, all adjourned to the central commons of the fort, where many tables were prepared with a bountiful feast of thanksgiving. The old war chiefs and their wives sat together, and the Cree chief, Grande Boisson, also joined them to discuss their hopes and fears.

The Scotts, Andre Bouvier, and Black Feather, Lucky Star and their husbands also sat together in one group. They spoke of simple things, family things, and friendship. Star, the wolf-dog, soon captured the attention of their children. Cricket and Messenger found a place on each side of the dog and hugged and petted him until he rolled over so they could scratch his belly. Some things never change.

23
The Secret Place

There are places that cross the boundaries of times and generations and tribes. They are what they are because they have been touched by the Creator in such a way that they grab on to a man's soul, and in these places, where they can be found, man reaches back.

Black Feather and Two Shadows found such a place on the highest crest of the Seven Sisters' Hills during the night of the showering stars and then again on their honeymoon at His high place overlooking the great lake, Gitche Gumee. Lucky Star had found her place at the swimming hole next to the colossal cottonwood tree. The war chiefs and enemies Gifted Hand and Buffalo Thunder had discovered it on the Buffalo Prairie, by the bones of the great and terrible beast, as they passed the peace belt one to another. Moon Song found it generations long in the love of her family. Shawn and Rylee Morgan Scott found their place revealed in the grandeur of The People; Andre Bouvier found it by giving back to the nations with the children's school at the French fort. What is it that they chanced to find, a place of wonder, to know the unknowable, to escape the confines of mind and body, to free their soul?

With each new child, the mysterious quest to find that place begins once again. Black Feather's and Two Shadows's son, Cricket, and Lucky Star's and Dusty Swan's daughter, Messenger, were poised to begin this journey.

Other movements were also under way. The tribes were established in their alliances and their territories. All of the nation's lands were overseen by one or more of the tribes, but new forces were at work. The French were pushing from the north and northeast, the English from the east, the Spanish from the southwest. All of the tribes were feeling the pressures of these irrepressible forces. The holy men and the chiefs of the tribes were earnestly calling out to the Great Spirit for guidance and for deliverance and protection from these daunting forces. Everything they were, everything they had known, all that they had hoped for had come to rest upon shifting sand.

The ancient legends of the Chippewa and the Lakota Sioux spoke of a holy place by the shores of Gitche Gumee called *Spirit Cave*. The People only sought out this cave in times of great need to seek a vision and find the will of the Great Spirit. The cave was never occupied for long without first praying and undergoing rituals of purification, for according to legend, ghosts protected the cave from wayward trespassers.

Burdened by the events pressing upon their people, the children's parents had decided to undertake a vision quest together to Spirit Cave. They joined up at the Chippewa stronghold and left as soon as the weather permitted and then arrived by the shores of Gitche Gumee in late spring. The first life-giving rains of the new season began to fall as they set up camp by the river flowing into the great lake.

"Do you know the location of Spirit Cave?" Dusty Swan asked.

His friend replied, "It is not many hours from this place, up the north shore of Gitche Gumee. According to Gifted Hand, you have to wait for a wind from the southeast. Then the Spirit Cave calls out."

"Sounds very mysterious," said Black Feather.

The group did not have long to wait. Overnight, the rain ceased, and the wind changed to the direction foretold by the legend. They broke camp, loaded their horses, and journeyed northeast along the Chippewa trail on the high ridge adjacent to the great lake. By midafternoon of the same day, they could hear a deep, haunting wail resonating upon the wind. They followed as the voice beckoned.

"When was the last time you were this excited?" asked Two Shadows.

"When you and I and the other young braves charged into certain death against the Pawnee war party," replied Dusty Swan.

Two Shadows smiled and remarked, "I feel the same way right now!"

Lucky Star challenged the men, "It doesn't take a Spirit Cave to know that we have to embrace each day with the ones we love and give thanks as though this was our last day."

Black Feather mused, "I think that our men need an elusive target. If they didn't have a mystery to chase, they would invent one." Both of the ladies laughed out loud, and Two Shadows demanded, "Quiet, you are drowning out the voice of the wind!"

Cricket and Messenger trailed along behind their parents, silently listening with the wolf-dog, Star. At last, they could see a large rocky promontory jutting out into the shining waters of Gitche Gumee. There were several holes in the rock face openings to Spirit Cave. The party dismounted, tied their horses, gathered some gear, and continued on foot.

"Look! There is a ledge that goes from the ridge top down to the big cave opening. It looks wide enough to walk on single file. When we are prepared to go, we can take the rope and tie off to each other," said Two Shadows.

"We will need to make torches," said Dusty Swan, and the group stopped on top of the ridge and did so.

"What about Star?" Cricket asked.

"We can't take the children or Star until we know that it is safe," said Black Feather.

"Children, you stay with the dog and our gear right here until we return for you," said Two Shadows. The children wanted to argue but did as they were bid.

The adults started a campfire for the children, lit their torches, and descended down the rocky path. The trail was actually quite good, about an arm length wide and not too steep, but it was three hundred feet to the rocks and crashing waves below. It only took about fifteen minutes to reach the cave entrance. The winds from the southeast abated, and the mysterious voice of Spirit Cave went silent.

Two Shadows entered in, and the others followed. Each held up their torch, and the walls of the cave came to life. They were in a large chamber, tall as a tepee and eighty feet wide. They could not see to the back, as it disappeared into darkness. There were ancient cave paintings all over the walls as high as a man could reach. There were naked men and women and scenes of villages and hunting and fishing and children playing. There were remnants of many campfires on the floor of the cave. Two Shadows said, "Let us go back to the children. We will gather our horses and make camp on top of the ridge. We must pray and purify ourselves before we remain for long inside the cave. We have seen that the trail is safe." All saw the wisdom of his words, and they returned to prepare camp and prepare themselves. The children asked question after question, and their mothers did their best to describe what they had seen.

"How does the cave sing?" asked Messenger.

"Who carved the pathway?" asked Cricket.

"Who made the paintings?" they both said at the same time.

"We may see tomorrow," answered Lucky Star, and then the men tended the horses, and the ladies prepared a meal of rainbow trout. After dinner, they all sat together on buffalo robes and watched the stars appearing over Gitche Gumee, and eventually, one by one, each of them drifted off into the land of dreams.

24

Spirit Cave

Dusty Swan and Two Shadows prepared the fire to carry their prayers aloft to the Great Spirit. The entire group encircled the campfire and fanned the smoke with their hands, up and over their faces. They chanted ancient praises to the Creator of all there is, asking permission to enter Spirit Cave—to seek his will for the People. To go into the cave for any length of time without these rituals of purification could invoke the wrath of the Great Spirit. According to legend, there were guardian spirits patrolling the cave. Only those pilgrims seeking the will of the Creator were allowed to leave the cave. Violators would be trapped there forever, their wails of torment heard whenever the southeast winds blew. Only those with a pure heart should dare to enter in.

"What do you expect to find?" Cricket asked his father.

"Whether or not we make war against the French and the English."

"And what about you, Father," inquired Messenger.

"I think war must come. I will ask for wisdom."

"How can we fight against our friends, people like the Scotts?" said Lucky Star.

"And which of you could destroy our friend, Andre Bouvier?" said Black Feather.

Two Shadows became angry and said, "All whites are not the Scotts or like our French friend at the fort. If war comes, the whites will force it upon us. We know the art of war, and they would come to regret it. We will not be pushed from our land. Enough talk—let's go now and seek for truth and wisdom.

The group tied the rope between them, lit their torches, and started down the ledge into Spirit Cave. The wolf-dog led the way. He paused twice on the path to look out across the expanse of Gitche Gumee and at the rocks three hundred feet below. The dog sensed danger, and Two Shadows intuitively picked up on the message from his faithful companion. Two Shadows turned to Dusty Swan and whispered, "Keep your musket primed and ready." Just as they were about to enter the cave, the southeast wind began to blow, and haunting howls once again issued forth from the cave.

"That's dreadful! Should we turn back?" asked Black Feather.

"Have faith!" said the little girl Messenger.

They entered the cave, and Star stopped, scented the air, and growled.

"I do not think that we are alone," said Two Shadows. He signaled to the rest of the group to stay by the cave entrance, and the men went forward into the large cavern to investigate. Star walked just ahead of them. The main cavern began to descend, the cave floor becoming like the staircase of giants with many layers of ledges. The men carefully picked their path and entered deeper and deeper. Suddenly, Star stopped, and the guard hairs stood up on his neck and back. He bared his teeth and growled. This was no false alarm; there was danger around the next bend in the cavern. Two Shadows signaled Star to be silent, and the three carefully made their way toward a hidden chamber off the main cavern. What a horror confronted them! There were human skeletons all over the cave floor, and a pair of green eyes looking down upon them from the ledge above. Suddenly, the monstrous eyes came closer, reflected in the light of their torches. The beast gave out a war scream that caused the men to shudder. The hideous apparition flew through the air, attacking, but Star jumped up and blocked the demon's airborne trajectory. They rolled over and over, locked in a fight to the death. "Hold my torch!" commanded Two Shadows, and he took aim at the beast that had Star by the throat. The musket exploded with sound and fury in a blinding flash and a cloud of black powder smoke. Star loosed himself from the death grip of the beast, shook his head, and raised his voice in defiance. He let out a victory howl that would have made his wolf ancestors proud. The large male mountain lion lay dead amidst a pile of human remains. At least one of the ghosts of the cave now had a face.

"Look at the size of this lion!" marveled Dusty Swan as he held the torches over the cat, black powder smoke finally dissipating.

Two Shadows reloaded his musket and then took back his torch. He thoroughly examined Star. The wolf-dog was bloodied in a dozen locations, but no wound was serious. "Let's haul the cat back to the mouth of the cave. Our women and children are sure to have heard the commotion."

"What has happened?" cried Black Feather.

The men told the tale, and then the women and children tended to Star. Then they gathered in a circle around the massive lion and viewed the beast with awe. The men would attend to the cat's hide later. The People never wasted any animal, even one as terrible at this. Perhaps Andre Bouvier could add the lion to his collection on the wall of shame, showing the just end of all premeditated killers, man or beast.

After the shock of their encounter subsided, the group began to survey the paintings on the cave walls. The artwork was masterfully accomplished and told many stories of the People. There were numerous prints of hands, both large and small. There were beautiful and graceful renderings of deer, elk, bear, and buffalo. There were depictions of entire tribes engaged in buffalo hunts. And there were scenes of battle between the tribes. People in ages past had also experienced fearful times of unrest. It showed in their paintings. But one thing remained the same: at the end of each wall, there were scenes of peace and villages going about the pleasant tasks of life. The paintings had encouraged each of them. The message was an affirmation. The Great Spirit would not forsake them in the end.

Star had disappeared into the cave, while the group had been preoccupied with the ancients' story art. The braves again directed the group to the cave entrance, and they returned to seek the wolf-dog. After descending past the lair of the mountain lion, about another hundred feet deeper into the cave, they saw the light from another cavern opening adjacent to the lake shore. There in the sunlight was Star, playing with two bear cubs. The mother bear was sitting on her rump, content to let her twins play and wrestle with Star. In some mysterious way, she had known that the wolf-dog was gentle and was allowing the play. Two Shadows and Dusty Swan observed silently and kept their distance. Finally, they turned and went back toward their families. They knew that Star would return in his own good time.

When the braves again rejoined their group, the children asked for Star. Dusty Swan replied, "He's paying a visit to the bear clan and will be back soon enough."

"We found what we came for. Let's go back to the top of the ridge and make camp for the night. We'll carry the lion with us," said Two Shadows.

The children were baffled at Star's absence, but if it was all right with the braves; well then, it must be so. After a sunny afternoon on the ridge, the winds stopped, and the wail from the cave ceased. Everyone sat around the campfire and awaited dinner for Star. As Dusty Swan had promised, the wolf-dog appeared, and the children practically smothered him with hugs. After the reunion, the group settled around the campfire once again, and the children climbed into their father's laps. They could no longer restrain their curiosity.

"So what did you find?" asked Messenger.

Her Father answered, "The Great Spirit has spoken. Trouble will come, and trouble will have its day, but in the end, the Great Spirit will honor those who truly seek him."

"What did you find?" asked Cricket.

Two Shadows looked upon his son and replied, "We met two beasts in the cave. One had an evil heart and came for us to take a spoil, and the Great Spirit acted through the wolf-dog to protect us until we were able to defeat our enemy. Another powerful beast was also in the cave, but its heart was good, and it intended us no harm. Star knew its heart and made friends with the bears. The Great Spirit has shown us the way. We will not seek war, but we will defend and protect our people. We will let the Creator of all there is reveal the heart of those who come from across the great waters."

The group spent another blessed night under the stars by Gitche Gumee. They were each thankful that the Great Spirit had revealed His will at Spirit Cave. The next day, they packed the lion skin and began their long journey home.

25
People and Ideas

News between the tribes of the region traveled as never before ever since the intertribal warfare had ceased. The French trading post and the children's school had become a clearing house of information. The braves traded their furs with Andre Bouvier and, at the same time, traded stories with the Frenchman, like that of the man-eating lion of Spirit Cave and the heroic deeds of valor by Two Shadows, his wolf-dog Star, and his best friend, Dusty Swan. The very same lion pelt now hung on the wall behind his trading counter next to the weapons of the renegade Métis brothers.

The Great Spirit was also moving across the nations. The braves and war chiefs, as well as holy men, were receiving visions and dreams, and seeking truth as never before. The news from Two Shadows and his party at Spirit Cave spread quickly throughout the tribes and became a confirmation. The Great Spirit had spoken the same message to all: diligence and patience were the watchwords of the day. At least for now, the voices calling for war had been stilled.

The seasons turned once more, and Messenger and Cricket joined the new class at Nations Academy. The French fort was busier than ever, as many new immigrants and would-be pioneer settlers were coming and going. The braves from all of the tribes in the region continued their fur trading as before but made more frequent visits to the fort, intrigued by the goings-on. The French trading post had become neutral ground where peoples of diverse

Indian nations, as well as whites from many countries of origin from across the great waters, were coming to do their business. At the same time, they were learning about each other, sharing ideas, meeting new people, and creating a realm of possibilities for all. The French fort had become a place of action, a new and powerful reality.

The children quickly settled into the classroom experience with Rylee Morgan and Shawn Scott. Messenger displayed an intuitive grasp of language and was learning to write in her own tongue and was beginning to understand basic expressions in French and English. She continued to impress the Scotts with her sharp memory, read to her a Bible story one time, and from that day on, she would repeat the crux of it without error. She was also becoming an accomplished storyteller and seasoned her tales with sound effects and well-timed gestures. The other Indian children enjoyed her gift and gathered around Messenger at recess to hear out her latest rendition. Cricket was also progressing well—in part because he had an advantage over the other children. His mother, Black Feather, could both read and write in French and English and had become proficient in Lakota Sioux and Cree. She had been reading Bible stories to Cricket from the beginning of his youth.

The school had added music to its language courses, and Cricket soon found his match with a wooden flute. The sound reminded him of the winds through the trees by Spirit Lake, and the breeze across the tall grass prairie. Cricket would sometimes play a song to accompany Messenger as she told her stories.

But as much as both of the children liked their school experience, whenever they were alone with each other, they talked of home and family.

Cricket asked, "What's the first thing that you will do next spring?"

Messenger replied, "Just spend time with my parents. I hope that my father is not gone too much. If he leaves, I will ask that he take me along. What about you?"

Cricket thought for a spell and then said, "I'm going to hang around with my dad and Star, go fishing, and visit my great-grandparents. Gifted Hand tells the best stories, kind of like you."

"Don't you miss your mom?"

"All the time, but it's not fitting for a young brave to say so."

"That's ridiculous!" Messenger huffed.

"Maybe," answered Cricket.

She looked at her friend and remarked, "I am glad that I'm not a boy."

"That's good, because I like you just the way you are," said Cricket, and he held out a hand to Messenger, and they walked hand in hand until other children came into view.

The other children relentlessly badgered Cricket and Messenger about their famed warrior fathers. The children reluctantly shared abbreviated versions of the battle stories, but they always ended them by saying that their parents sought peace. It was a letdown of sorts for the children as they craved the exciting action stories. Disappointed, the children turned to Andre Bouvier. When he was not busy trading furs, he would allow them to come in by his trading counter, and then he would spin wild yarns about the wolf-dog and the renegade killers, the Métis brothers, and about the man-eating lion. He made epic heroes of Cricket's and Messenger's fathers. The children devoured these wild orations, and they could not understand why Cricket and Messenger were holding back. The warrior brave's children each understood that peace was elusive, and they had learned from their mothers and from Moon Song that words carried a power of their own. If you desire war—speak of war. If you seek peace—speak of peace. Both children tried to honor the hearts of their father's by their words. Cricket and Messenger preferred to share the tale of how the old enemies, Buffalo Thunder and Gifted

Hand, brought about an end to the war between the Lakota Sioux and the Chippewa. The other children heard out the stories but seemed far more interested in the part played by the bones of the mysterious monster on the Buffalo Prairie, where the warrior chiefs had first passed the peace belt. Messenger repeated the account, as relayed by Buffalo Thunder, that of the Jesuit priest from Spain and about the war in heaven that had resulted in terrible beasts being thrown down to the face of the earth. Once again, the children savored the action.

The children's interest in the bones of the monster had not escaped the attention of Rylee Morgan and Shawn Scott. They, too, were intrigued by the tale. A notion was beginning to come to them: what about gathering the class together at the end of the term, as soon as the weather allowed, and undertaking a field trip to the Buffalo Prairie? The Scotts knew the key participants of the drama, and they could ask them to lead their party to the site of the mystery beast. The remainder of that winter term, they proceeded to make the arrangements. In the spring, they would adventure west to discover the truth of the terrible beast on the Buffalo Prairie.

26

Signs and Wonders

THE CRUSADE TO JOURNEY WEST on the Buffalo Prairie, to investigate the mysterious and terrible remains of the legendary beast, was unprecedented! The party consisted of forty-five souls: eighteen school children, five warrior braves from each of the three tribes as armed escorts, Two Shadows's and Dusty Swan's families, the three tribal war chiefs, Moon Song, and the Scotts. The wolf-dog Star would lead the procession, with each person, young and old, upon their own horse. The size of the expedition was sure to be seen by other hunting or war parties on the Buffalo Prairie, but the Scotts and the warrior chiefs were confident that the size of their group would discourage any mischief by their enemies, the Pawnee and Shoshone. Also, the adult men were well armed. Each carried a musket and the tribal warriors their traditional weapons as well. Many brought their war lances to hunt buffalo, as the large group would have to take some provision on the trail.

The groups from all three tribes—the Lakota Sioux, the Chippewa, and the Cree—rendezvoused at the Sioux stronghold. There they assembled for an excursion of unknown duration upon the western plains. The Sioux offered up a dozen pack ponies, each trailing a travois loaded with tepees and enough possibles to set up a temporary camp at the target sight on the Buffalo Prairie. The expedition was outfitted as never before to make certain that the children in their care would be safe and secure. It would be unthinkable not to return the children safely home to their villages, and any misfortune could have dire consequences. On the other hand, a successful spirit quest for knowledge by each of the participants could bode well for future relations among all of The People. The stakes were high indeed and as auspicious as the powwow that had brought about an end to the war between the Sioux and Chippewa. The holy men and warrior braves of the Sioux held a feast in honor of the expedition. There they performed ceremonial fires and drummed and danced until well into the night, the events ending in prayer songs for protection and the leading of the Great Spirit. The following day, the party ventured westward.

Messenger and Cricket rode toward the front of the expedition, following closely after the wolf-dog. Buffalo Thunder, the first to discover the bones of the legendary beast years ago, led the way. It was a windless, clear horizon and the noon sun sent undulating heat currents rising from the tall grass prairie, playing tricks upon the senses. It was proving difficult to look out across the prairie; the motion of riding a swaying horse coupled with the shimmering curtains of heat became disorienting. No one liked the feeling of not being able to trust their own senses. Butterflies began to flit through the rising thermal currents, disappearing in and out of view in the liquid mirage of enchanted air. Messenger began to feel uneasy. She said to Cricket, "I am troubled. I don't know why, but I have a sense of dread."

Cricket quickly scanned the horizon all around them, clutched his bow, knocked an arrow into place, and replied, "I don't see anything, and the wolf-dog has not broken his stride. Maybe it's just the heat mirage."

"No. I feel very strongly that something is about to happen."

Cricket looked around once more then rode back to join Two Shadows. "Father, Messenger has had a premonition. We should alert the warriors in our party."

Without any hesitation, Two Shadows let out a war whoop and rode through the group to raise the alarm. He instructed the braves to encircle the children in case of attack, and then he rejoined the war chiefs. Cricket drew close to Messenger. Suddenly, the wolf-dog stopped and stared off to the southwest. Everyone halted. A hideous high-pitched whine came out of the far horizon, like that of steam whistling from a boiling pot. Then they saw it coming! Parallel to the horizon, a burning ball as large as the sun hovered just one hundred feet above the ground. It appeared to be suspended there, moving slowly but ever closer. Everyone was silent, but the horses began to react. The sight had spooked them. The people reined in their mounts to steady them. Then the great fiery ball fell from the sky and crashed silently into the earth. A great billow of smoke and dust rose high above the horizon, and one minute later, a shock wave flattened the tall grass all about them and tumbled many from their horses. A thunderclap of exploding sound reached them with a deafening roar! Panic had overtaken most of the children, and there was shouting and screaming. Two Shadows and the other warrior braves quickly reacted and helped the children to retrieve their horses. They assured everyone that the event was over and that everyone was safe. After order was restored, the men gathered together to assess what had occurred. The question was raised by Grande Boisson, the Cree war chief, "What was it?"

By virtue of her proximity to the front of the party, Messenger had heard the question, and she answered boldly, "It was a falling star."

Rylee Morgan and Shawn Scott had assembled with the war chiefs and heard Messenger's response. Shawn Scott concurred and said, "Yes, without a doubt, it was a meteorite: a shooting star. It only appeared to fly level with the earth for a ways because its path was quartering toward us. We just witnessed the death of a star."

Grande Boisson posed, "Is it safe to continue on our journey, or is this an evil omen?"

Gifted Hand spoke, "We can see the smoke and dust rising from the impact. It's straight ahead and on our path, so let's go and see this sight." After a short discussion, it was agreed that the danger had passed, and now everyone wanted to examine the crash site. Terror and dread had quickly been replaced by human curiosity—the reason in the first place for this entire expedition.

The star had actually been farther away than anyone had suspected, and they traveled many hours to reach the location. They arrived late in the afternoon and were met by an astonishing sight. There was still smoke rising from the impact crater, but the shockwave had cleared away all the peripheral grass, negating a wild prairie fire. There was a long furrow, a ditch-like gash in the earth. It trailed off for a half mile to the southwest, appearing like a great finger pointing toward a crater of blackened earth fifty feet wide, surrounded on three sides by a raised wall of dirt. Nestled in this amphitheater of mother earth, half buried, lay the still smoldering shooting star. It was a pockmarked sphere as big from front to back as a war pony. Some children impetuously wanted to climb down into the impact crater and touch the star, but the adults quickly forbade them. It was still far too hot to touch. The adults marshaled the children away a safe distance, and after some discussion, they decided to stay the night and examine their find in the morning.

Moon Song, Black Feather, and Lucky Star prepared the evening meal for the entire group, and after supper, the braves built a large campfire, and everyone gathered about to discuss the events of the day. All the Indians were familiar with shooting stars, but none had witnessed one such as this. The Scotts had some knowledge of astronomy and shared what they could about meteors, meteorites, and comets. But they, too, had never seen one do what this one did. At the end of their speaking, Shawn Scott concluded, "We have all witnessed history here today. This was a star the likes of which man may have never seen before."

What Shawn Scott had said gave Moon Song an idea. She turned to Messenger and asked her, "Do you remember the story of the three wise men that followed the star?"

Messenger replied, "Yes, I remember."

"With the war chief's permission, would you tell us that story?"

Messenger nodded, the chiefs quickly agreed, and she asked everyone to move closer together by the fire. She began, "Once long ago and in a land far away, three wise men who were kings and scholars saw a great star moving across the night sky. In those days, the appearance of such a star could mean only one thing: a great king would soon be born, and the star would mark the way. They followed the star for many days until they came to a village called Bethlehem. The star stood still and shown down upon a stable, where horses and other animals were lodged for the night. But there was also a man and his wife, and the woman had given birth to a son. They were in the stable on the hay because there was nowhere else for them to stay. The wise men came, following the light of this star, and brought gifts to the new baby, befitting those of a great King. The man grew up to be a King of kings, the one true Son of the Great Spirit, and was named Jesus, or in their tongue, God with us. The end."

All the children and many of the warrior braves had questions, but Moon Song said to them all, "There will be time enough on our journey to ask your questions, but now it's time for the children to sleep. Thank you, Messenger, for telling us about this other great star of Bethlehem."

Many in the group, including the adults, wondered if this star that had lodged on the Buffalo Prairie, in their witness, was itself a messenger from the Great Spirit.

27
A Day to Remember

With the dawn, five buffalo appeared upon the horizon: a bull, two cows and their calves. The Cree braves were the first to spot them, and they eagerly asked permission from the war chiefs to give chase. Grande Boisson, Cree war chief, said to his young warriors, "Yes, but you must take one of Buffalo Thunder's braves along."

"I will go with them," offered Dusty Swan, who was experienced with pursuing this big game.

Gifted Hand cautioned the group, "Make it a quick hunt—take but one buffalo. We cannot place our children at risk. Strike quickly and stay close. Return at once if I fire my musket."

The Cree braves were as excited as children; this was to be their very first hunt for the king of the prairie. Some of the braves loaned the Cree their war lances, and Dusty Swan let them lead the hunt. He said, "Ride past the herd and drive them back toward our people. Surround the bull and strike with both lances." Dusty Swan purposed not to participate in the kill unless the bull threatened to unhorse a rider. He wanted it to be a Cree hunt alone.

The Cree hunting party worked together skillfully, separating the bull from the cows and calves and then delivering their spears right on target. Their trophy bull came to rest upon the prairie. The braves dismounted and gathered around the bull. They sang a prayer song to accompany him upon his next journey. After a few moments, Dusty Swan asked the Cree to remove the cape from their prize, and then he returned to camp and retrieved a pack horse and travois. There would be a celebration feast for all by midafternoon.

The hunting party returned just in time for breakfast, and as the group sat together, the Cree braves shared the tale of their very first buffalo. The war chiefs appreciated that Dusty Swan had held back and given the Cree braves the glory of the hunt. Then the entire group removed to the crater of the shooting star. The dark, nickel/iron sphere had cooled sufficiently to allow the excited children to touch it. The surface, still warm, appeared like liquid boiled in a pot with a hundred pockmarks and bubbles. There were some streaks on the sides where the star had come into contact with rocks in the earth as it slid to a stop. The children climbed down into the ditch, spread out, and found palm-sized hunks of the star along its glide path. The remnants were reddish bronze, in contrast to the ink-black dirt, and easily seen. What a prize they were! Each of the twenty school children, including Messenger and Cricket, found their own piece of the celestial orb. This story would bear repeating for generations to come, and the children appreciated these once-in-a-lifetime artifacts. The Scotts gathered a saddle bag of the meteorites to display at the school and saved the largest specimen for Andre Bouvier for inclusion with his other treasures. The group spent hours examining the shooting star and the wound it had carved in the earth. Later that same day, the men gathered brush and deadwood for a splendid bonfire, and the women prepared a sumptuous feast of fresh buffalo steak, wild rice, and boiled potatoes. The entire group reveled in the manifold blessings of the day: fresh meat, a banner bison hunt, and their very own shooting star.

As the group settled in for the afternoon, they began to reflect. Cricket posed the big question, "Does everything that happens in life have a reason?"

"What do you mean?" replied Gifted Hand.

"Like the shooting star, did it come for a purpose? Is it a message, or was it just its time to fall from the sky? And why now? Why did it fall in front of us for us to find?"

"Let's see what the others think. Buffalo Thunder, do you have an opinion?" asked Gifted Hand.

"I think some events have a greater meaning. It seems to me that life is a collision of opposing forces."

Moon Song spoke, "The dark gives way to the light. The cold gives way to the warmth. The things of this life give way to the things of the spirit."

Two Shadows remarked, "All things are not knowable by man—some mystery remains."

Grande Boisson was intrigued by Two Shadows and pressed him, "Did you find this truth in the Great Spirit's book of words?"

"No. It's in everything around us."

Rylee Morgan Scott remarked, "Seeking God is the true joy in my life."

Gifted Hand asked, "What happens when you find your Christian God?"

Shawn Scott replied, "You can have peace."

Messenger finally spoke up and asked, "Do you mean peace between The People and the Europeans or inner peace?"

Shawn Scott was caught off guard by the girl's question, looked down, and just stared into the campfire. No one in the group had that answer. After a lengthy silence, Buffalo Thunder said, "Night is upon us. Let's turn in and start our journey once again…fresh in the morning."

Gifted Hand added, "Maybe some of our answers lay ahead on the Buffalo Prairie."

The western sky put on another brilliant display—a magnificent meteor shower—and the children watched in wonder. They talked among themselves well into the night, their bodies finally surrendering to the fatigue of the high excitement of the day.

Pondering the profound under an enchanted night sky finally led them to sleep, one by one.

The wolf-dog, Star, had nestled between Messenger and Cricket, who always remained close to each other. Their mothers, Black Feather and Lucky Star, observed their children. Lucky Star whispered to her best friend, "The shooting star has indeed delivered a message. Look at how it has brought us all together."

Black Feather responded, "The Creator of all there is has joined together with us on this journey. What wonders will He yet perform?"

The women shared a sense of overwhelming peace as they observed their children and the wolf-dog falling asleep in the waning light of the campfire and under the celestial dome of shooting stars.

28
The Dig

The vastness of the Buffalo Prairie was matched by the dome of heaven and by one more natural phenomenon—the insatiable curiosity of the human spirit. Love and war, setbacks, and ambitions all paled in significance to the invigorated intellect of man.

The day broke calm and clear, and the group once again headed west to continue their quest for enlightenment. By midday, Buffalo Thunder spotted the sun's reflection upon the skull of the beast. As the mounted contingent drew closer, the skull loomed ever greater in size. The people arrived, dismounted, and silently approached.

"Here it is," said Buffalo Thunder, "our great mystery!"

Everyone in the party stood before the skeleton and then began to mill around to take in the proportions of the immense beast. Some of the braves stepped away from the group to gather materials for a campfire. The women and school girls prepared lunch from the available stores: buffalo steak. With the meal ready, Rylee Morgan Scott called out, "Come and get it!"

The conversation was lively, and the food fit for a king. The children began to ask question after question about the creature, and finally, Moon Song asked Buffalo Thunder to share the legend of his youth. He retold the Jesuit priest's tale about the war in heaven and how the rebel angels were defeated and cast down to the earth in the form of great and terrible beasts. Some of the children had heard of the story before, but here, in the presence of the actual creature, the tale came alive to them. One of the children asked, "Chief Buffalo Thunder, you heard this story as a child, do you think it still true?"

He responded, "The passage of time never changes truth."

Gifted Hand stared across the campfire at the skull of the beast. The rising convection currents above the blaze seemed to make the skull move, and the sight was terrifying indeed—even to this old man of war. The six-inch dagger like teeth were designed for attack and death, a sobering sight. He finally came up with a notion: "We have enough people and horses and time, why don't we dig up the beast, release it from the earth and stone and take it back to the French fort? Can you imagine? People from every tribe and from all nations would want to see it."

"Do you think it possible?" asked Grande Boisson.

Shawn Scott said, "We can do it! I have shovels, picks, hammers, and chisels on my pack horse. I can document the location of each bone in my sketchbook as we recover them from the sandstone, number each specimen, and we can reconstruct the skeleton perfectly back at the fort. The bones have turned to stone, so we should be able to chip them out without damage. What a grand project it could be—think of it! We could add science to our language studies. The beast could stand once again as it did here on the prairie. What a gift to all of The People!"

Dusty Swan asked, "What about disturbing the burial site of the creature? Will this offend the Great Spirit?"

There was much discussion by the adults, and the consensus was that no one could be certain. The war chiefs and the Scotts deemed that it was worth the risk, considering the knowledge that might follow the reconstruction of the beast. Curiosity once again ruled the day. Even so, out of respect for what they were taking, many in the group left small offerings of grain, beaded jewelry, arrowheads, and other small personal treasures. Soon, in front of the skull, there lay an Indian blanket covered with gift offerings. Messenger even left her piece of the shooting star, a most prized possession. One by one, without prompting, the people left their tokens. They honored the Great Spirit for the gifts that he had bestowed upon them.

The group set about the task at hand, each person, young and old, helping from dawn to dark. Finally, one late afternoon, the last piece of the tailbone was recovered. The group settled around the campfire next to the burial site of the creature one last time. After dinner (buffalo steak was losing its appeal), they began to relax and share their impressions of over one month of group effort on the Buffalo Prairie.

"I never thought we could do it," said Grande Boisson.

Shawn Scott replied, "When people work hand in hand, there is little that can stand in the way."

"What have we learned together?" asked Gifted Hand.

Cricket weighed in, "The Great Spirit has spoken to us through the shooting star and the great beast."

"What did He say?" Buffalo Thunder prompted.

Black Feather replied, "Signs from heaven cause us to seek the will of the Great Spirit."

Buffalo Thunder pressed, "What is this will?"

Messenger spoke, "The presence of the Great Spirit has brought love to all in our group. The star and the creature were only signs of His presence."

Two Shadows said, "We don't know for certain about the star or the creature. The Great Spirit has demonstrated to all of us the power of mystery. We need mystery—it drives us forward. Our expedition will soon end, but our hunger and thirst to know truth and the will of the Great Spirit continues on. For all of us, another journey has begun."

The next day, the expedition was loaded and on the way back to the French fort. Each horse and travois was heavily laden; together they carried the complete skeleton of the beast. Not one bone, large or small, was missing. After a journey of eight days, the expedition arrived at the French fort amidst a clamor of excitement. Everyone turned out to greet them, marveling at their find. Andre Bouvier, once acquainted with the Scott's intentions, exclaimed, "We will build a special structure to house and display the creature, with classrooms for further study!"

After a short stay and many celebrations at the fort, the braves from the three tribes were charged to escort the school children back to their respective villages—and what stories they would have to share. Each child possessed a piece of the shooting star (Messenger's meteorite had been replaced by the Scotts), and they all could attest with a certainty that the great beast exists. It would be displayed for all of The People to see at the French fort.

The Scotts thanked everyone for their splendid behavior and cooperation; this endeavor would serve to bind all of the participants together. Their epic adventure made them fellow partakers and makers of history. The school children and the adults from all three tribes found it hard to say good-bye—none wanting the adventure to end. One thing for certain, all the children were enthralled at the prospect of returning to the French fort, to the Nations Academy, with the coming fall term. The Scotts were invigorated by the events and eager to discover new truths with these very same children.

Messenger thought to herself, as her family departed, whether the Great Spirit would be served by the aftermath of their summer expedition on the Buffalo Prairie. Also, would it draw the people together in such a way that they could have the peace that everyone desired? Only the coming seasons held the answers.

29

Saying Good-bye

Life in the Chippewa village had always been sublime—The People touched by a special harmony with all of nature and by walking with the Great Spirit. But now, after the recent events of years just lived, there had come to be a special richness. Gifted Hand and Moon Song were great-grandparents, blessed by family and the fullness of years. The warrior chief was proud that he had been allowed to see the blessings of peace. His one time archenemy was now counted among his best friends. The adventures they had shared. Such signs and wonders upon the Buffalo Prairie and an even greater wonder—brotherhood. Moon Song had helped show the way of love and respect for all of those close to her and to be careful with their words. Seems as though the more she gave her love away, the more she had to give. The seasons were drawing to a close for Gifted Hand, and he sensed it—but never was a man more thankful or content. He allowed ample time to spend with his granddaughter, Black Feather, who he loved more than his own life. She, too, sensed the change in seasons and loved upon her Grandfather.

"Let's go for a duck hunt!" he would say to Cricket and Two Shadows and the wolf-dog, Star. The father and son would put aside their activities, and they spent as much of their time as possible that last fall season with Gifted Hand. Cricket loved to hear his great-grandfather's stories, and over the weeks that followed, he learned all about his tribe and the joys of the hunt and how to be a true human being. It was a bittersweet time for

Two Shadows, for he knew this would be the end of hunts for Gifted Hand.

When Gifted Hand was alone, he contemplated his life. He had deep regrets for the men that he had killed in battle, especially Screaming Eagle, the true grandfather of Two Shadows. But there is scarcely a man alive that does not carry a burden for his actions. He had loved Moon Song completely, without reservation, and he regretted the possibility of leaving her alone. He prayed to the Great Spirit to protect and provide and bless her always. There was no need. She was already in the palm of the Creator's hand. Her love for all and her faithfulness had connected her to the Great Spirit since the days of her youth. And as soon as she had been introduced to the Jesus, by her friend Rylee Morgan Scott, she had embraced him as her own.

Toward the end of the season of falling leaves, Gifted Hand was moved to ask his true love for one last favor. "Would you join me in climbing the great hill of the Seven Sisters? I would like to watch the ducks coming and going to Spirit Lake."

Moon Song replied, "Of course, my husband. Let me first gather a blanket and some kindling for a fire." She did so, and the two old people slowly made their way to the summit. When they reached the mountain top, Moon Song spread the blanket, and Gifted Hand built a small campfire. There was a gentle breeze from the southeast, and it carried the smoke away behind them. The fire became a heartwarming companion. The ducks were arriving in an ever-increasing cascade. They swirled in great, dark clouds over the lake. Some of the flocks came in from behind them, just above their heads, close enough to reach out and touch as they descended from the northern sky toward Spirit Lake. The redheads, canvasbacks, and bluebills appeared like gems on a necklace, the bright sun causing their colors to explode upon the senses. Their wings cut the air and whistled their joyous song of fall.

Gifted Hand finally said, "I am quite weary."

Moon Song said ever so softly, "Just rest for a spell. Stretch out in front of me and lay your head in my lap."

She stroked his face gently, sweeping his snow-white hair from his closed eyes, and she began to sing her farewell love song. Then Gifted Hand peacefully and contentedly joined the migration home.

Within moments, the wolf-dog Star appeared at her side. He raised his head to the sky and gave out a lonesome cry. The mournful wolf song resonated with the wind and carried to the village. Two Shadows, understanding, rallied the braves. They became an honor guard – escorting Moon Song, bearing their fallen leader home.

30
Hall of Science

The summit of the Seven Sisters Hills was considered a high holy place and not a place of burial. Gifted Hand's tribe carried him instead to the sacred hills on the south side of Spirit Lake, and he was laid to rest among the other chiefs of renown on a special burial mound. Great reverence was taken in the selection of this site, and he was placed carefully, laid out with precision with the other chiefs. Together they formed a council circle, like the spokes of a wheel, so that for all eternity, the former war leaders could watch over and commiserate on the affairs of men. Even in death, they were charged to intercede on behalf of The People with the Great Spirit. The news of Gifted Hand's parting soon spread to the French fort and then to all the tribes in the region. Even faraway enemy tribes—the Pawnee and Shoshone to the west, and the Comanche to the southwest—heard of his passing. Among the Indian tribes, their own greatness could be measured in the strength of their enemies and among all the tribes, Gifted Hand commanded respect. Even his enemies suffered the loss—the passing of a worthy adversary.

The seasons moved on, and so did The People. Messenger and Cricket returned to the French fort to begin their second term at Nations Academy. Cricket brought with him, at the request of Moon Song, the white peace belt. This emblem of the great reconciliation between the Lakota Sioux and the Chippewa, engineered by Buffalo Thunder and Gifted Hand, would occupy a place of honor among the treasures displayed by Andre Bouvier.

He would add the noble history of the peace belt to his cannon of great stories told to all who would listen at his fur trading counter. The turquoise-studded treaty emblem hung just next to the shelf displaying the shooting star.

The Scotts were thrilled to be reunited with all the children, especially Cricket and Messenger. They, too, loved Gifted Hand and had been devastated at the news of his death. It was still too painful to talk about for them all, so they just embraced at their reunion and plunged forward upon the joyous task at hand—their second term together.

The superintendent of the French Fort, Andre Bouvier, was true to his word, and the structure to house the great beast of the Buffalo Prairie and the attendant classrooms were well under construction. The building would be completed by midterm.

Shawn Scott had prepared part of the existing classrooms as a workshop. The first piece of the skeleton of the beast was brought forth from storage, from its temporary location in the fur trading warehouse. The huge skull took center stage and was the first specimen scheduled for cleaning and restoration. When the expedition initially retrieved the bones from the sandstone on the Buffalo Prairie, all the sandstone had not been removed from the skull in the field. The fine cleaning would take more careful work in the controlled environment of the workshop. So the Scotts dedicated part of each class day to the restoration efforts. On the weekends, many of the children volunteered their free time to work on the skull. By midterm, the skull was made perfect, and it was transported to the newly completed exhibit hall. Next, all of the bones were moved to the new building and science classrooms, and rapid progress was made restoring the remainder of the skeleton. By the end of their second term, the skeleton had been thoroughly cleaned and restored to its original condition. The bones of the beast had long ago come to rest on the silt-laden bottom of an ancient lakebed, and now, after miracles and hard work, they gleamed in the sunlight on the floor of the great hall at Nations Academy.

The entire class gathered in the new building, which had been named the "Gifted Hand Hall of Science," on the last day of school. Rylee Morgan Scott said to the class, "Our adventure together on the Buffalo Prairie has continued. You have not only excelled in your language, music, and math studies, but you have accomplished great things on the new science display."

Shawn Scott addressed the children, "This coming summer and fall, in your absence, I will arrange all the bones on the floor of the great room. Each bone will be put in its proper alignment, according to my field drawings and notes. Next, I will drill holes in each segment of the skeleton so that by strategically placing steel rods, your class can build the creature from the ground up next winter term. It will stand again, as it did in its lifetime on the Buffalo Prairie. What a project it will be, and I hope to see each of you back here for the start of our third term."

Cricket asked, "Do you think it possible to finish rebuilding the creature next winter?"

"With many hands working together, it is possible and consider how proud the war chiefs will be, including Gifted Hand."

Messenger offered, "Would it be permitted for some of the adults from the three tribes to work with us to assemble the creature?"

"That's a great suggestion. I will ask the war chiefs. The adults can stay free of charge at the lodge," said Shawn Scott.

Rylee Morgan added, "I'm sure it can be arranged. Thank you, and I pray that all of you will have a safe journey home and a blessed summer and fall with your families. See you next term."

Everyone said their good-byes one to another and awaited their escorts, the braves from each of the three tribes. The warriors arrived, and the children began to assemble. Messenger and Cricket held back until the last and found a quiet place near the gate, out of sight of the others. They hugged until their arms hurt, and finally, reluctantly, they parted. Their gaze followed after each other as they rejoined their respective groups. Then deep in thought, they commenced upon their separate journeys.

31
The Wicker Woman

The Great Spirit once again was about to demonstrate that he had a way of sorting out events and people. The very same day that Cricket had returned home from the French fort, a most unusual visitor appeared at the Seven Sisters Chippewa village. She came alone, riding upon a chestnut mare, trailing a travois with all her worldly possessions in tow. The warrior outriders of the village escorted her to the lodge of Gifted Hand. Moon Song, Two Shadows, Black Feather, and Cricket emerged to meet her.

She introduced herself, still astride her pony, saying, "I am Wicker Woman. I have heard of the passing of the noble chief, Gifted Hand. A friend has sent me with a message for his widow."

"What is this message?" Two Shadows demanded.

Moon Song spoke out, "Let her first come down from her horse and rest and eat after her journey. Wicker Woman, I am Moon Song, the wife of Gifted Hand. Welcome to our lodge."

The elderly woman struggled to dismount, and Cricket ran to her and helped steady her. She placed her hand upon his shoulder, smiled, and said, "Such a fine young brave. You must belong to Gifted Hand."

"He was my great-grandfather, I am Cricket."

Two Shadows went to her pony and unstrapped the travois, propping it against the buffalo-skinned wall of Gifted Hand's lodge. Then he led the chestnut mare to food and water, tethering her to a stake in the ground.

Moon Song ushered their guest into the lodge; everyone remaining was introduced, and then they shared a simple meal and refreshment.

The two older women sat next to the campfire, and she began to tell her story. "I was born into a tribe very far from here, in the deserts to the southwest. Our people lived as one with our beautiful, but dry, land. We raised sheep, cattle, and horses. Over the ages, our people were given the knowledge of how to raise corn in the arid land. We could get a good corn crop—but only about every two out of three years. We lived in homes made of adobe clay, covering a scaffold formed of sticks and grass. Our roofs were made of the same and supported by poles, which we had to bring from distant mountains. Our homes or pueblos were warm in the winter and cool in the summer. We learned many useful crafts, taught to our ancient people by the Great Spirit, and became experts at weaving clothes of wool and the making of sturdy baskets from willow whips and the ribs of cactus. But our greatest gift was the making of ceramic bowls and containers. We depended on these containers to store our food grain and our water to sustain us in the years without crops. We learned the complex method of firing our clay and the components of special paints and glazes, making our bowls both beautiful and dependable. Our family owned some ceramic bowls that were made by aged generations and still fit for service."

Two Shadows interrupted and resumed his questioning, "Why have you come now to our village?"

Moon Song, who rarely became angry with her family, admonished her grandson, saying, "Please allow Wicker Woman to continue."

"My people were living in harmony and happy times. But then warriors from the north raided our pueblo village, surprising us, taking horses, killing our braves, and stealing our women. I was one who was kidnapped. We traveled far from home, and I lived for many years with the Comanche raiders. It was a hard life, and

I will not speak of their cruelties. Then once again, other enemy raiders from even farther north came to steal ponies, and I was taken away, this time, to a Cheyenne village. They were unlike the Comanche and kind to captured women—even welcoming. The Cheyenne and Lakota Sioux had become allies, and I married a Sioux warrior. I lived in the village of Screaming Eagle. My husband was killed in warfare between the Lakota and your Chippewa braves. They met on the Buffalo Prairie, as hunting parties, and the braves were thrown headlong against one another. I continued to live with the Sioux, and I am familiar with many of your friends: Buffalo Thunder, Dusty Swan, Lucky Star, and Messenger. I have often heard the stories of your family. Buffalo Thunder asked me to go to Moon Song and show her the crafts of my native people. This is his way of honoring the memory of his friend and brother, Gifted Hand. To answer your question, Two Shadows, I was sent as a companion for Moon Song and as a teacher to your tribe."

Moon Song looked upon Wicker Woman and discerned that her account was truthful. She said, "You are welcome to our tribe, and you will live here with me in the lodge of Gifted Hand."

Black Feather and Cricket also expressed their welcome, and Wicker Woman was adopted into their family that very hour—ending her long and mysterious journey. This was to be her final home.

Over the coming weeks, she came to know every man, woman, and child at the Seven Sisters camp, and her gentle ways and kind spirit soon made her a favorite. She especially enjoyed the mornings with Black Feather and Cricket. Black Feather would feed her wild birds; Cricket would sing and talk to them, and Moon Song and Wicker Woman would join in attendance with the others from the tribe. They all sat together and listened to a new story from the Bible. Black Feather made the mornings a rendezvous with the word of God, and all were touched.

After one morning session, Wicker Woman remarked, "Do you know, at the Lakota Sioux village, Messenger also shares a story from the Creator's book of life every morning by the lodge of Buffalo Thunder? Her stories and your stories are in one accord. Black Feather, you and your Grandmother have touched her deeply."

Cricket looked off to the west and longed to be with Messenger again. He asked, "How was she when you last saw her?"

Wicker Woman placed her hand once again on Cricket's shoulder, and answered, "She was thinking of you."

The birds began to congregate around the feeder, enticed once again by Cricket's calling. The Wicker Woman said to Black Feather, "I was able to spirit away seed corn when I was first captured, and in later, kinder years, I was able to grow many varieties of corn. One is very special, with small kernels and many colors, and especially attractive to wild birds. I will make a gift of this corn to you."

"How wonderful! I will plant this corn at once, thank you, Wicker Woman."

That summer was an amazing time in the village. Wicker Woman taught the Chippewa people all her secret methods of making the ceramic bowls and containers and also how to fire them perfectly in an outdoor kiln. Then she taught them her knowledge with the wicker baskets, a skill which had become her namesake. All in all, she had been a true blessing to the tribe and a most valued friend, sister, and companion to Moon Song.

That exciting summer and fall passed quickly, in part because of the knowledge imparted by Wicker Woman, but now it was again time for Cricket to return to school. He could hardly wait to see Messenger once again and to resume their work at the Gifted Hand Hall of Science.

32

In Spirit and Truth

THAT FALL, SOMETHING OCCURRED THAT no one had planned or expected. Thanks to Wicker Woman's presence, many in the Chippewa village were producing pottery and basketry of an exceptional quality. The process that she had taught them was so enjoyable that many in the tribe had produced an abundance of articles, amassing an inventory of more containers than they could ever use. Trade had always been a small part of each tribe's way of life, so it seemed fitting that the braves take the surplus ceramic and wicker baskets along while they returned the school children to the French fort.

Other things had taken place. The many varieties of corn that Wicker Woman had brought with her had been distributed among the tribe. The People were quick to plant and nurture this corn. The growing season complete—the fields were ready for harvest. What an amazing and bountiful crop it was! Never had the Chippewa seen such corn. The ears were full and robust, and the fall harvest turned out to be the best ever.

Without any conscious design, a movement had arisen in the tribe. The people had taken heart in the works of their hands, becoming inspired, and were producing as never before. It was not only the province of corn and pottery and wicker baskets, but their skills also manifested in other traditional native crafts. The women were making many beadwork masterpieces: clothing and moccasins and jewelry, beaded handbags, and backpacks; and the men were turning out birch bark canoes, fish weir baskets, and braided leather ropes of an exceptional quality. They had experienced a renaissance, an outpouring of creative energy across the entire village. The summer activities had been nothing short of miraculous!

When the braves and the schoolchildren departed for the French fort late that fall, they each carried behind their mounts a travois loaded with trade goods. Special, extra long travois were constructed to receive five birch bark canoes. When their train of horses, people, and goods arrived at the fort, the people in residence were astonished! From where did all these amazing trade goods come?

Andre Bouvier instantly seized upon the opportunity and quickly made a place for all the wares at the mercantile store and also at his fur trading warehouse. He knew that the canoes would sell out immediately, and he asked the braves to carry a message home that he would purchase all the canoes that they could produce. The other goods, placed at the mercantile, would also sell out quickly. There was a steady influx of people now in the fort, and they would be hungry for these necessities. The articles of beaded clothing, moccasins, jewelry, and especially the beaded handbags would catch the eye of the pioneer womenfolk. They were worth the price, practical, beautiful, and maybe even a little wistful.

The braves remained one night, their dual mission accomplished, children and goods delivered intact. Andre Bouvier had purchased the entire lot, at a very handsome price. The braves asked but one favor the morning of their departure. They wanted to see the infamous bones of the creature one more time. Bouvier and the Scotts were quick to accommodate them, and together, they toured the Gifted Hand Hall of Science. What a summer and fall it had been for them all. Then the braves set out for their village, as there was much to do to prepare for the coming winter.

Over the next few days, all children from the three tribes arrived at the fort. Cricket waited expectantly for the return of the Lakota Sioux children—one in particular. The morning came, and Messenger appeared. She was even more radiant than he had remembered. She had changed since last year, and Cricket could discern the young maiden appearing in her supple form. He was practically speechless.

"What's wrong with you? Can't you even say hello?"

"Welcome back," he managed to say.

"How did you like Wicker Woman? Isn't she something?"

"There is no one else like her."

"Truly. I really miss her. Next to my mother and father, and Buffalo Thunder, she is my favorite person in our tribe."

"She's a little mysterious."

"That's part of her charm. How are your parents and Moon Song?"

"They are well."

"How about the wolf-dog?"

"Ah, he is slowing down a little. He's getting older, you know."

"Yes, it seems like great dogs, like Star, are never with us long enough. I pray to the Great Spirit often to give your wolf-dog an extra long life."

Cricket took her by the hand, and the two young people spoke no more. They headed across the commons toward the buildings at the Nations Academy, Cricket no longer self-conscious that other people could see them together holding hands.

"Greetings, children, are you ready for your third term?" asked Shawn Scott. Before they could answer, Rylee Morgan Scott surrounded them with a bear hug. She kissed them both, and it was truly a joyful reunion.

The third year at school seemed to speed by like a running deer. By the end of term, the creature from the Buffalo Prairie had assumed his former stature in the great room of the Gifted Hand Hall of Science. He was bigger than anyone could have imagined and quite terrifying. Shawn Scott had done a masterful job of positioning the drill holes to receive the steel mounting rods, and the skeleton had taken shape flawlessly, looming thirteen feet from the floor to the top of his head and forty feet long from his teeth to his tail. It was a good thing that one of the braves from each of the three tribes had remained behind to help construct the beast. Their strength was needed to heft some of the huge bones into position. Now the school term and the beast were completed.

The entire group gathered together to view their towering creation. Shawn Scott addressed the group, saying, "I have been in contact with scientists from England and France, sending drawings of our creature. They have replied, and I am told that our beast has a name and is known among modern science. It has been determined that it is called a dinosaur, specifically, *Tyrannosaurus Rex*. In the language of science, Latin, the name means, 'Terrible King.'" Supposedly, this creature represents the most fearsome predator of its day."

The children surrounded the beast, craning their necks to fully appreciate its proportions. Finally, Messenger asked what many in her class were wondering, "Does this news from the men of science mean that the legendary account by the Jesuit priest, as reported by Buffalo Thunder, is untrue?"

Rylee Morgan Scott answered, "Not in the least. Children, here at Nations Academy, we have always tried to teach you with the precepts of the Bible, in spirit and in truth. When properly understood, science never opposes the Word of God. Because scientists have placed a name upon this creature, it does not change that it was part of God's great design. Have no fear that science will ever rise above the Word or plan of the Great Spirit."

Shawn Scott had some parting words: "Thank you one and all for your fine work this past term. What you have learned in class and what you have built here in the hall of science will come to serve all of the people for generations to come. As you leave now, share what you have learned, and we will see you once again next winter for your final and last term."

Over the next few days, the children were met by their escorts and began to leave the fort. The Scotts pulled Messenger and Cricket aside, and Shawn Scott said to them, "You have both excelled in all of your classroom studies, and we wish to ask you, with your parent's permission, to accompany us at the completion of your fourth term as we travel to England, Scotland, and France. We will be gone for nearly a year, and we will experience a world of excitement as we share about your people and your great accomplishments. Please take your time and consider your decision wisely."

The children could hardly wait to put the matter to their parents. They hugged the Scotts and then rallied their escorts to speed them on their journey home.

33

Kingdoms

Cricket wondered if summer could possibly be as exciting as last year. He wondered if he could even concentrate from day-to-day as his mind and spirit were in another place and with another person and completely focused on journeys yet to come. He needn't have worried; life has a way of commanding our attention. Every day has the potential of becoming a new adventure, worthy of all there is inside of us.

One enchanted and sunny morning—after the wild birds had been called into attendance and fed with colorful Indian corn, after Black Feather's latest Bible story about the kingdom of God—Wicker Woman began to speak. She shared a story, and the twenty people in attendance hung upon her every word. "You have just heard an account by the spirit of God himself, about His kingdom in heaven. Cricket, next spring, you and Messenger will join your friends, the Scotts, in visiting kingdoms across the great waters. Let me tell you now of legendary, but real, kingdoms of the Indian people's, far to the south of my desert homeland. As a young girl, I often heard the stories when strangers from the south came to trade with our Pueblo people.

"Throughout the ancient of days of long ago, the ancestors developed great cities rising high above the ground and made from hewn stone. These cities were places of power for the kings and places of worship and science and great wealth. They were cities filled with gold and silver and gemstones and turquoise. Many, many people lived in and around each city. Their people had mastered the science of agriculture, and they had great crop fields surrounding these cities as far as the eye could see. They had even learned the secrets of the stars and the seasons and could predict the perfect time to sow their crops. They came to understand numbers and applied this knowledge to all things, especially in designing and constructing their buildings. They even built roads between the cities and brought water into the cities from miles away. They also brought water to their fields and had a crop in the dry years.

"These kingdoms lasted for hundreds of years. But something happened. The power and riches corrupted the kings, and they became cruel. Warfare broke out from one kingdom to the next, and some of these kingdoms fell—never to rise again. The great glory of the Mayan civilization was lost to time. One new kingdom gradually emerged, reclaiming the former grandeur of the Maya. They called themselves the Aztecs, and they were a most powerful and brutal kingdom. No other tribe or city-state dared to challenge them, and they became the undisputed power for generations. But then something happened once again. Men from across the great waters, from a kingdom called Spain, invaded the kingdom of the Aztecs. The men from Spain were warriors, and by war and by the diseases that they brought with them, they prevailed and destroyed the Aztec kingdom. Closer to my home and far north of the Aztecs, another kingdom arose and became the Anasazi, the ancestors of my own tribe as well as other tribes in our southwestern deserts. The Anasazi built palatial cities in the sides of mountains and were known as the cliff dwellers. The Spanish came to war against the desert tribes but were defeated and turned back.

The Anasazi ruled the deserts for many generations, but their kingdom, too, mysteriously disappeared. So you see, kingdoms come and go. We Indians also had our kingdoms. Even the kingdoms from across the great waters will rise and fall. Power, and greed, lust for wealth, and cruelty, and forgetting our way with the Great Spirit will someday be the end all of man's earthly kingdoms." Wicker Woman had an end to speaking.

The entire group was silent; it was so much to take in. Cricket finally asked, "What about the kingdom of God, will it stand?"

Black Feather responded, "It is the one kingdom without end." Then the group disbanded, going on about their varied summer day routine.

Cricket could not get Wicker Woman's account out of his mind. Who was she, really? Was she an angel or a prophet? He had listened to Black Feather's Bible stories for years, and he had heard that angels sometimes took the form of men and visited The People. He also knew that the Lakota Sioux war chiefs and holy men had seen visions and dreamed dreams of white men who would someday triumph over the Indian Nations and occupy and control the land. If Wicker Woman's words were true, maybe this is the Indian people's future. But if it is true, will the white man's kingdom, too, fall someday, and would the great circle of life once again turn to his people? These big thoughts were too heavy to carry, so Cricket called out for Star. They geared up, loaded their canoe, and set out upon Spirit Lake. Fishing has a way of lifting heavy burdens.

34

Sweet Air of Home

Shawn and Rylee Morgan Scott faced a critical choice: what route should they determine to take ship with the British? They had counseled with Andre Bouvier, who was always well informed by his far-flung trading partners. The news was ominous: sporadic warfare between the Eastern Indian tribes and the English colonists had begun. The most direct overland route would land them in the territory of the eastern bands of the Chippewa, of the Three-Nation Pact, who were also fighting the British. The northern route via the great lakes was no better. Flare-ups with the Iroquois Confederacy precluded this route to Boston. Another route—down the Mississippi and then up the Ohio River and then cross-country to Jamestown—was also a hornet's nest of Indian resistance. The only safe route remaining was the Mississippi River all the way to New Orleans. The Scotts could engage a party of Lakota braves to deliver them safely to the French staging camp, a gateway to the Mississippi at Lacrosse. There they could purchase passage with the French fur traders and join with a flotilla of thirty-man cargo canoes headed for the Gulf of Mexico. Once in New Orleans, they could take ship to London.

The children returned once again to the fort—Cricket and Messenger bearing permission to accompany the Scotts to Europe in the spring. They began making their plans. The children came well prepared, with extra clothing and camping gear neatly stowed in beaded backpacks. Their tribes had provisioned them well, understanding the importance of their undertaking. The tribes had blessed them and commissioned them as emissaries to the powers of Europe.

The Scotts were responsible for teaching twenty children that final term—and not one child would be shortchanged. They had the presence of mind to keep their upcoming trip separate. The days would belong to the class. Their evenings and weekends were set aside for Cricket and Messenger and for special planning. In the evening sessions, the Scotts prepared an itinerary for their travels in Europe. They also went over all of their research materials, paintings, and records of the tribes and their way of life. The sessions also became an intensified training of Messenger and Cricket on the customs and history of England, Scotland, and France. By the end of the final term and with the coming of spring, they set out for England.

The trek and the boat ride to New Orleans was long and arduous but took place just as planned without any serious hardships along the way, thanks to the Lakota braves and the French voyageurs. The first leg of their mission was complete.

The ocean voyage on the British merchant ship, *The New Resolute*, was also uneventful and without any significant bad weather to impede their progress. Four months after departing the French fort, they arrived in London. The children had already been away from their families for eight months, and though excited to see Europe, when alone with each other, they talked only of home.

When the news spread about the Scotts and their contingent of Sioux and Chippewa Indian children, their reception was nothing short of a stampede. Newspapers, diplomats, academicians, and dignitaries thronged to meet them. They quickly became the toast of Europe, with everyone wanting an audience with this once-in-a-lifetime delegation. After two weeks of lectures and introductions at Oxford University, they received a royal invitation to meet the king.

They were treated with all the pomp and circumstance reserved for heads of state and warmly received by King George III and his wife, Charlotte of the house of Mecklenburg-Strelitz. The kings and queens of Europe had intermarried for generations to forge political alliances between sometimes hostile neighbors, and everybody was somebody's cousin. The Scotts and the children bowed and were introduced to the monarchs. The king adored children, and asked them to come forward and stand with him and his wife. He greeted them on behalf of all his royal subjects, and then he asked them to share their personal ambitions. He listened attentively as first Messenger and then Cricket told of their hopes and dreams. When the children had made an end to speaking, the king's wife held out a hand to Messenger and smiled. "How old are you, my child, and from what Indian nation do you hale?'

Messenger took an immediate liking to the queen consort and answered, "I am almost twelve years old, and my people are the Lakota Sioux, known as the master horsemen of the Buffalo Prairie."

Then King George put the same question to Cricket, and he responded, "I am twelve, and my people are the woodland Chippewa. We live among the hills, lakes, and forests given to us by the Great Spirit."

Charlotte turned her attention to the Scotts and asked if she could see the sketchbooks of Shawn Scott. Reports of the thoroughness and quality of his Indian paintings had preceded them. The king also studied the renderings as his lady turned the pages. "Oh look!" she said, "Here you are, Messenger, making a woven basket with your mother." More pages were turned, and the king observed, "And here you are, young man, hunting deer with your father. I, too, love to hunt deer."

The meeting was most cordial, lasting for over an hour. Finally, the king asked the children if they had any questions for him or for Charlotte. Cricket was silent for a moment, but Rylee

Morgan Scott encouraged him, saying, "Just speak your heart to the king." Cricket took a deep breath and said, "My people want peace, but your people want our land. How are we to live and survive together?"

The king placed his arm around Cricket's shoulder, and in a very kind tone of voice, he responded, "Even kings do not have all the answers. There are great and terrible movements afoot in Europe and the Americas. Perhaps we need guidance and even intervention from our eternal Father. My personal desire is for peace, but the times seem to have taken on an inertia of their own design. Events have moved ahead of the desires of kings. I wish that I had something more encouraging, but know this: your presence and deportment here today have won over our hearts!"

The royal lady asked Messenger, "Child, do you have a question or comment?"

Messenger replied, "I have been taught by my people…all kingdoms that forsake the responsibilities and brotherhood of man will fall by the injustice of their own designs."

"My child, your words are most alarming, and I fear prophetic. Your people are indeed wise. Please, will you do me the honor of corresponding with me? I wish to designate you as a valued advisor to our realm."

"I will, Gracious Lady," replied Messenger. Then the audience came to an end, and the Scotts and their children started their extended journey to Scotland, then to France.

Their stay in Scotland was a holiday with the Scotts and was the children's favorite respite to the journey. They had time to walk alone in the heather to smell the perfume of the Scottish countryside and to watch the brook trout. The fish leaped in a spray of wondrous colors to nimbly snatch the caddis flies midair. Messenger and Cricket were now forever linked on the same path and could no more be separated than a person from their own heart. Next they traveled to France and were soon brought into the presence of King Louis XV and his queen consort, Maria of the house of Leczinska.

The French embraced a great love and appreciation for the Indian nations and, unlike the British, did not seek to conquer Indian lands. The French treated them as sovereign nations and lived with the tribes—often intermarrying with the Indians. Cricket and Messenger were treated as far-flung sons and daughters, and their conversations did not have the pointed edge that the children had experienced with the English. In France, they lived at the royal palace and were treated to every enjoyable diversion by the royal household. They loved France and were, in turn, loved by France.

Messenger and Cricket had both been asked to correspond with the French king. He valued their reports and their honest appraisal of conditions in the New World.

Shawn Scott found the French scholars and scientists eager to embrace his paintings as well as Rylee Morgan's book of translation. They were also wildly compelled by the news of the Tyrannosaurus Rex—many wanting more news, and some, even desirous of a trip to the French fort to collaborate with the research on the find at the Gifted Hand Hall of Science. A door had been opened, and a marvelous exchange of ideas was sure to follow.

The Scotts and the children had accomplished their mission and opened dialogs with the rulers of Europe. They had also opened doors with Oxford University, and with the preeminent scholars and scientists of France. There were no more heights to scale, so they made the necessary arrangements to return home. It was time to return, and after four and a half months of marathon travel, they stood once again with their people and breathed in the sweet air of home!

35

THE WHIRLWIND

THE SEASON WAS LATE NOVEMBER when the young people and the Scotts returned to the Seven Sisters Chippewa encampment. Snow had blanketed the area. The Scotts and Messenger had decided it prudent to winter with the Chippewa. This fortuitous decision was an elixir to Cricket's spirit. His lovely Sioux maiden and his mentors would be constant and welcome companions until spring.

Messenger, Rylee Morgan Scott, and Black Feather stayed in the lodge with Moon Song and her companion, Wicker Woman. Shawn Scott bunked with Two Shadows, Cricket, and the wolf-dog. The entire group assembled frequently for meals, and whenever together, they discussed recent events. The other braves in the tribe also attended these informal councils. They had the time now—thanks to the extra trade and revenue produced by the village's crafts and canoes—and were not compelled to leave camp, as in the past, to service extensive trap lines.

The braves were most interested in the Scotts and the children's reports. They wanted to know all about the conflict between the eastern tribes and the British, the military capability of the armies in Europe, and, most importantly, the European's intentions.

The Scotts passed along all that they had heard about the eastern wars. Of most interest to the braves was the report that their eastern brothers, the Ojibwa (as part of the Council of Three Tribes) and their allies, the Ottawa and Pottawatomie, were in open warfare with the English. The fight was a long distance off, but the first blood had been spilled, and the words stirred the braves. It seemed that the war all had feared had begun in the east.

Two Shadows asked about the strength and numbers of the foreign powers in Europe. Cricket answered his father, "Their standing armies and ships of war were ever present on our journey. The main seaport cities in both England and France were filled with soldiers, and the harbors crowded with gunships. This was true to both England and France. Europe is an armed camp, and the English and French are poised for battle. Their wars have reached our shores, and they are fighting in Canada and in the eastern reaches of our own lands."

Two Shadows considered Cricket's report and then spoke aloud his thoughts, "I wonder how we would fare against such an army."

Cricket soberly replied, "We might do better to fight against the wind or the rain or against time itself!"

His statement alarmed the braves, and they sang out one after another:

"What if they take our land?"

"What if they kill our game?"

"What if they destroy our forests and our waterways?"

Moon Song could see that passions had been kindled, and she said, "Do not forget the Great Spirit. He is greater than any tribe or any nation or any army. Let us eat now and then go out separately to seek the will of the Creator."

The council meetings were suspended for several weeks so that the people could come to terms with the unsettling events and, once again, command their emotions. Cricket followed the lead of his father, Two Shadows, and spent much time isolated in the sweat lodge, purifying himself and seeking guidance. The women were also praying. War had a very real face to them; death and injury was no stranger to any of their lodges.

Death with honor was acceptable in the warrior creed, but it was not the women's creed. They longed for the blessing of future generations.

Cricket's body was exhausted; the hours of fasting and steaming in the sweat lodge had removed the toxins and numbed his thoughts. His mind was suddenly set free! He entered into a vision more real to him than life itself.

> I saw a great cyclone approaching, a whirlwind as large as the sea. It was a twisted, dark mountainous range of clouds. The forests of the east stood against the wind and were snapped off. The reeds of the lakes bowed down before the wind and were spared. Two great herds of buffalo stood against the wind—one herd on the southern plain and one on the Buffalo Prairie—and most were swept into the sky and carried away. Few were spared. Then I saw snow geese, and they took flight and disappeared to the north and were spared.
>
> The winds blew and blew and blew. Then I saw a gray owl that was nesting upon a single egg. This egg did not hatch. She tried again, and still, the next egg did not hatch. For seven seasons in a row, she had no success. Finally, in the eighth season, her egg hatched, and she reared up a healthy baby once again. This baby owl was an end to my vision.

Cricket quickly left the sweat lodge, dressed, and sought out Messenger. He repeated the vision, and she wrote it down word for word. Then she asked to be alone and spent the next hour in Two Shadows's lodge. Cricket grabbed a blanket and his flute and sat on the snow next to his father's tepee, and he began to play a most inviting refrain. The wolf-dog, Star, appeared and lay at his feet. It was a warm and sunny winter day, and the people were moving about the village. Hearing the song, the people, including all of his friends and family, retrieved their blankets and joined Cricket.

Finally, Messenger appeared and said, "I have been in prayer, and the Great Spirit has revealed to my mind the meaning of your vision. Would you like to hear it now?"

Many in the crowd, including Two Shadows and Wicker Woman, replied yes. She began, "The storms, as great as the sea, are the Europeans. The trees that were severed before the wind are the tribes of the east that went to war with the whites. The reeds that bowed down and survived are the Chippewa. The buffalo that stood against the wind and were nearly destroyed, with only a remnant remaining, are the Cheyenne of the southern plain and the Lakota Sioux of the Buffalo Prairie. The snow geese that escaped to the north are the Cree.

"The owl that you saw represents all the tribes in time, for seven generations The People must endure and suffer under the power of the Europeans. In the eighth generation, our life and our spirit will be released and restored to us." Messenger came to an end of her interpretation. She looked at Cricket, and he nodded in acceptance of her words. She said, "We should share this vision with all The People."

Cricket responded, "It will be done. Could you please write down what the Creator has revealed to your spirit?"

"Of course, I will do as you ask."

The prophecy of the vision and its interpretation would eventually spread among the tribes. Only time could reveal its worthiness.

Two Shadows looked upon Messenger and his son. He said, "Cricket, you have earned a new name worthy of respect. From now on and ever after, you will be called *Gray Owl* in honor of your successful vision quest with the Great spirit and your meetings on our behalf with the kings of Europe." Two Shadows joined the hands of Messenger and Gray Owl together then raised his right hand above them both and blessed them. He prayed aloud, saying, "Together, may you fashion the future of our tribe."

About the Author

My name is Stephen Leonard Bjorklund, and I am a common man, an ordinary American. I have made my living as a builder and a craftsman and have been blessed by family—worthy wife, four children, and six grandchildren.

I have always had an interest in nature and the outdoors, and this leading has drawn me to become acquainted with the rich history of the American Indian, the quintessential outdoorsmen. I also love artwork and the writing of stories. *Chippewa Suns* is my first novel but not my first book. Over a period of forty years, I have also written two collections of short stories, *The Golden Pocket* and *The Homestead Collection*.

I hope that you enjoy this fictional account of two Indian families from two rival tribes set in the 1730s to the 1760s. To my way of thinking, this is the way it could have been.

About the Artist

Diane Bjorklund, the author's sister, was born in Minneapolis, Minnesota, and her teachers recognized early on that she was a gifted artist. She went on to study at the Minneapolis Institute of Art. Diane paints in the classic style of the old masters, and is adept at composition and the use of color. Her paintings also capture a mastery of the interplay between light and dark. Her paints also reveal a story, and it was indeed fortunate for the author to engage Diane to illustrate *Chippewa Suns*, as she was already deeply involved with other commissioned art projects.

Diane resides in the San Diego area and often paints by the Pacific Ocean. Her paintings demonstrate her abiding love for people and the human form, but she also has a gift for wildlife, horses in particular, and landscapes. She masters all with her unique artistic vision. This brother/sister collaboration was seen by both as a high point in their creative careers.

Bibliography and Credits

The credits are listed by subject and then followed by sources:

1. The Council of Three Tribes (Ottawa, Pottawatomie, and Ojibwa) and King George III and Charlotte of Mecklenburg-Strelitz. Source material: Gerry and Janet Souter, *The Founding of the United States Experience.*
2. King Louis XV and Maria of the house of Leczinska. Source material: http://en.wikipedia.org/wiki/Louis_XVI_of_France
3. The Lakota Sioux circle of life, the medicine wheel, and the four virtues. Source material: www.prairiestar.com/culture.htm.
4. Ancient Native American civilizations: Maya, Aztec, Anasazi, and Pueblo. Source material: Gascoigne, Bamber. HistoryWorld. From 2001, ongoing. http://www.history.net.
5. The Spanish conquest of the Aztec. Source material: http://en.wikipedia.org/wiki/Spanish_conquest_of_the_Aztec_Empire